PHOENIX RISING

THE COMMANDER OF THREE OF THE MOST POWERFUL MIND-CONTROLLED, SPACE-AGE DRONES EVER CREATED, TURNS FROM THE SUPREME HUNTER INTO THE HUNTED

MARK T. WELLINGTON

*For the love of my life
and the center of my universe,
my darling wife,
Mirabela.*

DEDICATION

To Tom Clancy,

It is with deep gratitude and admiration that I dedicate this book to you, the man whose incredible storytelling ignited my passion for writing and gave me the courage to find my own voice.

From the moment I picked up one of your novels, I was entranced by your keen ability to weave intricate, thrilling tales with precision and heart. Your masterful storytelling not only engrossed me but also planted a seed of inspiration within, urging me to explore the world of writing for myself.

As I embarked on my own journey as an author, your unyielding dedication to the craft served as a constant reminder of what could be achieved through perseverance, discipline, and a true love for storytelling. Your work provided a beacon of hope as I struggled to find my footing and my own unique style.

Through your novels, you taught me the importance of authenticity and the value of connecting with readers on an emotional level. You showed me that stories have the power to transcend the boundaries of time and space, allowing us to tap into the human experience in ways that are both intimate and universal.

It is because of your influence that I have been able to tell my own story and create worlds of my own, unearthing the beauty and complexity of the human spirit. For that, I will be forever grateful.

Thank you, for inspiring me to dream, to write, and to never give up. Your legacy will continue to live on through the generations of authors and readers you have inspired, and your stories will remain a testament to the power of the written word.

With heartfelt gratitude,

Mark

CONTENTS

CHAPTER 1
KNOCK, KNOCK

A TORRENTIAL DOWNPOUR batters the city as an ambulance careens down rain-slicked streets under a hail of gunfire. Lightning flashes illuminate the dark sky, followed by the growling of thunder. Oncoming traffic passes in a blur as Sam Reynolds maneuvers the ambulance like a man possessed—driving as if the devil himself were on his tail. His EMT training didn't include evasive maneuvers under intense gunfire, but he's learning now.

"Shots fired! Shots fired! This is EM-223 northbound on I-495! Request immediate assistance!" Sam screams into the radio.

"10-4, EM-223. Dispatching all available units to your location," returns the dispatcher. "Hold on, Sam. Help is on the way."

"Tell 'em to move their ass! I don't know how much longer the three of us can last out here!"

In the midst of the chaos, Sam steals a glance at the medical bay where his fellow EMT, Janice, is frantically cutting open the jumpsuit of a semi-conscious man on the gurney.

Air Force Major Tony Simmons is powerfully built with

rugged good looks like he's stepped right out of a recruiting poster. Smart as he is tough. Einstein and Chuck Norris stuffed in a hand grenade.

"How's that guy doing, Janice?" Sam asks.

"G.S.W. to the right shoulder. Through and through," Janice Farmer replies, her hands steady despite the adrenaline pumping through her veins. The wound is clean and small. Most likely from a high-speed rifle round. Before she gets a better look, Sam takes a hard left sending equipment and supplies flying. Tony's losing blood fast.

"Rasheed, put some pressure on the wound while I wrap his shoulder."

Rasheed Smith is no stranger to gunfire. Tall as he is wide, he's never missed a meal. Raised on the streets of Baltimore, there wasn't a day that went by that didn't involve violence. But trained soldiers on a mission to kill are a different story. He reaches for thick gauze and applies a little too much pressure, bringing Tony fully awake.

"Ahhh . . .!" Tony groans.

"Damn it, Rasheed,"—as she backhands his shoulder—"not so hard!"

Gunfire erupts from behind, riddling the left side of the ambulance with holes. Everyone ducks. Sam takes a hard right avoiding a bus as he runs through a red light.

"Dammit! Who the fuck is shooting at us!" Rasheed demands.

"Ask him!" Sam gestures toward Tony.

"How about it, G.I. Joe? Who the fuck are they?" as he gets in Tony's face, the fear in his voice palatable.

Gritting his teeth through the pain, "I don't know. Al-Qaeda, Russian Spec Ops. You wanna pull over and ask?"

The pursuing military van pulls alongside the bullet-ridden ambulance and tries to muscle it off the road. An oncoming 18-wheeler forces it to retreat while the commandos are firing, their shots barely missing the rear tires.

"I need power," Tony states.

"What? What for?" Rasheed demands.

"Don't ask me why! What kind of power runs this equipment?," pointing to the defibrillators.

Rasheed grabs Tony by the collar. He's had enough. "Look, motherfucker, you better lay the fuck down before I put you down!"

A large .45 caliber pistol instantly appears in Tony's hand. He presses it to Rasheed's forehead. The big man freezes, his eyes wide with surprise.

"Don't make me kill you."

"OK, man, OK. Be cool, be cool."

Rasheed slowly raises his hands. Janice is shocked to see the gun to Rasheed's head. She shudders out, "It's . . . it's . . . a standard 120 volts."

"Good. Unplug that defibrillator and pass me the power cord."

Janice fumbles but finally hands Tony the cord. He places it near the base of his neck. Two sensors embedded in the back of his head begin to pulse bright blue.

"What the fuck . . .!" says Rasheed.

"Calm down, big boy." Turning to Sam, "How much time to the hospital?"

The ambulance lurches as he frantically maneuvers to avoid oncoming traffic. "Fifteen minutes!"

Tony slams his hand down hard on the gurney.

"We're not going to make it!" Tony states desperately. He realizes he can't do this alone. He turns to the stunned E.M.T.

"What's your name?" Tony asks.

"Rasheed."

"Listen to me, Rasheed. Those commandos are going to kill us all if I can't make this connection."

Tony expertly flips the .45 around and hands it to him.

"I need you to keep them off our ass. Can you do it?"

Surprised by the reversal, he looks into Tony's eyes and

knows he's deadly serious. The only way to live through this is to fight back. "Yeah, man. Gimme that shit."

"Single shots, right at the driver. Stay down behind that crash cart. Got it?"

Tony throws him an extra magazine.

"Yeah, got it." Rasheed kicks open the ambulance doors and lays down, covering fire. The van swerves and repositions.

Tony braces himself against the wall of the ambulance, preparing to establish a neural connection with the Devastator 5 Advanced Combat Drones: Zeus, Apollo, and Athena. As he concentrates, a complicated series of numbers and geometric shapes flash in blue neon within his mind, activating the cybernetic interface embedded in his brain. With the cutting-edge blend of neuroscience, cybernetics, and quantum computing, his neural signals are swiftly intercepted, amplified, and transmitted securely to the Devastators. The advanced quantum processors within the drones interpret Tony's commands with incredible speed and precision, allowing him to control their artificial intelligence at the speed of thought. The video feeds and tactical displays from the drones appear in his mind's eye; his eyes glaze over a bluish hue.

"Initiate start-up sequence," Tony commands.

ZARAFSHAN AIR FORCE BASE, UZBEKISTAN

A deep underground military base hidden under the mountains in western Uzbekistan houses the secret research facility of the Synaptic Network Center (S.Y.N.C.), a clandestine research facility dedicated to cutting-edge drone technology. The subterranean complex is a maze of cavernous hangars connected by maglev transports that glide silently through the dimly lit passages. Colossal steel beams stretch up into the darkness, forming a skeletal framework that supports a vast, domed ceiling. Suspended from the beams are an array of powerful floodlights that cast eerie shadows across the metallic floor. At the heart of this underground lair, the Devastator 5 drones slumber like fearsome birds of prey. Technicians in white lab coats move with quiet efficiency as they prepare the formidable war machines for their next mission, their fingers dancing over touchscreens and adjusting delicate components. The drones' shimmering, adaptive skins pulse slowly as if breathing in anticipation.

Professor Jonathan Blackstone, Chief of Technology, stoops through the entrance of the hangar—his lanky frame better suited for a basketball court than a top-secret military installation. As he surveys the scene, the sleek dragon-like weapons spring to life. Their powerful engines send racks of equipment skittering across the hangar floor, and Blackstone's eyes widen in disbelief.

THOUSANDS OF MILES AWAY, Tony establishes a connection to the Devastators and prepares them for an emergency flight.

"Initiate flight sequences. Activate GPS tracking. Navigate to my position. Engage supercruise. GO!" he commands.

THE DEVASTATORS slowly move forward as technicians frantically scramble out of the way. Regaining his composure, Blackstone sounds the alarm and races toward the hangar doors, barking orders to nearby soldiers.

"Close the doors! Close the doors! We can't let them get away!"

One of the soldiers turns to see the Devastators pick up speed as they make their way to freedom. He punches the control that starts the sequence. The massive steel structures slam close just in time.

———

Tony, viewing the scene through the drones' LED cameras, realizes the only way out is through. He activates their weapons systems, and in unison, the Devastators open their weapons bays. "Knock, knock!" he smirks.

———

Each drone fires a single, devastating sonic pulse, blowing the reinforced hangar doors off their tracks, and hurling them onto the security vehicles outside. With the path now clear, the Devastators glide past the flaming wreckage, making their way to the runway for takeoff.

———

S.Y.N.C (SYNAPTIC NETWORK CENTER) HQ, RESTON, VIRGINIA

The Electronic Warfare Operations Center buzzes with activity, its dimly lit room filled with state-of-the-art equipment and monitors displaying real-time data. At the heart of the action, an electronic warfare officer (EWO) sits confidently, his eyes scanning the complex array of high-tech displays.

Suddenly, a flashing blip materializes on a map of the eastern seaboard, immediately drawing the EWO's attention. He swivels in his chair, turning to the duty officer. "Colonel Morris, sensors have picked up the Devastator 5 encrypted control signature."

Colonel Morris brings up the display on his command console, his face set in a grim expression. This is the moment they've been waiting for. "Do we have a positive I.D.?"

"Yes, sir. It's Major Simmons."

Morris's gaze shifts to a shadowy figure standing in the corner of the room. With a single, decisive nod, the figure grants permission. "Configure a neural digital spike (NDS). Track the target, then fire."

"Yes, sir!" the EWO replies, his voice filled with determination.

On a nearby display, the Devastators' movements are tracked in real time. The EWO's fingers fly over the controls, his face a mixture of concentration and urgency. "Sir, I can't configure a precise strike before the Devastators are airborne."

"Stop him now! I don't care if you fry the whole city!" Morris barks, desperation creeping into his voice.

"Yes, sir!" the EWO responds, his hands moving even faster over the dizzying array of buttons and switches. A bar display fills to indicate a 100 percent charge. High above the Earth, a satellite moves into position and opens its bay doors. A pulse cannon glows, its energy building as it takes aim.

"Spike fully charged. Firing in 3 . . . 2 . . . 1"

THE SLIDE of the .45 pistol locks back, signaling the end of the magazine.

"I'm out!" Rasheed yells, back.

The pursuing black van moves in for the kill. Tony, his mind racing, moves to the front of the ambulance. "I have to get them to safety. They're almost free . . ." he mutters, his voice distant and strained.

"What are you talking about?" asks Rasheed.

"I think he's going into shock," Janice answers back.

"We need a full tox screening on this guy; whatever he's on, I want some!"

The satellite fires a massive blue energy beam that pierces the surrounding cloud cover with its intensity. The massive electronic pulse radiates out from the ambulance and kills all electronic devices in a 10-mile radius. Tony grabs his head and screams in pain as the NDS (electromagnetic pulse) hits his cybernetic interface and disconnects him from the Devastators.

IN AN INSTANT, the engine of the pursuing van dies, sending the vehicle careening out of control. It smashes through the guardrail of a bridge and plunges into the icy waters below.

ON THE TARMAC, the Devastators spool up their powerful engines preparing for takeoff, then abruptly initiate their shutdown sequence. They sit idle as the confused technicians run up, wondering what just happened.

"COLONEL, THE ELECTRONIC STRIKE WAS SUCCESSFUL," the E.W.O. reports. Colonel Morris turns toward the dark figure as he leaves the control room to an awaiting helicopter on the roof.

WITH ITS SYSTEMS FRIED, the ambulance hurtles into a line of parked cars. The vehicle flips onto its side, grinding to a halt amidst twisted metal and shattered glass. Tony drags himself out of the wreckage. "Is everyone OK?" he asks, his voice weak.

The EMTs emerge from the ruined ambulance, nursing cuts and bruises.

"I'm good," Sam confirms.

"Me too," Janice adds.

"What the fuck . . . yeah," Rasheed says, surveying the carnage around them. "Really, man, who the fuck are you?"

With a dark threatening look, Tony takes the gun from Rasheed. Having lost his connection to the Devastators, seething rage builds inside.

"I'm a trillion-dollar weapons system that's being hunted by fucking madmen . . . If I don't stop them . . . our whole country, everything . . . it's over."

Rasheed stares at Tony, at a loss for words as Tony tucks the .45 back into his waistband.

"Any more questions?"

Silence

"Good."

Rain falls mercilessly onto the black asphalt, reflecting the dim glow of streetlights. The relentless downpour is accompanied by an eerie silence that blankets the once-bustling Alexandria suburb. Tony surveys the devastation around him. Dead silence as bewildered people begin filtering into the street. Not a single light in sight.

"You guys better clear out of here; it's not safe. This is only the beginning," Tony warns. He turns and stumbles down a nearby alley, the blueish glow from his neural interface fading as he disappears into the shadows.

CHAPTER 2
A DANGEROUS GAME

72 HOURS EARLIER

A YOUNG UZBEK BOY, clad in ragged grimy clothes, guides a small group of goats along a dusty road. In the distance, a deep rumble grows louder, causing the boy to cover his ears and huddle his goats close together. A pair of F-35 stealth fighters streak overhead, their powerful engines roaring as they bank sharply, preparing to land at the sprawling U.S. airbase on the horizon.

Lieutenant General Adelay Smith, director of the Devastator 5 program, stands in his office, which offers a commanding view of the combat drones in the hangar below. A jagged scar runs along his jawline. His piercing blue eyes focus intently on an array of holographic displays hovering over his desk.

The General's aide, Captain John Pitterson knocks and then enters.

"Director, you have a priority Q Level call on the SATCOM." A perturbed look crosses the general's face.

"Thank you, John"—just as Captain Pitterson reaches the door—"Have you seen Dr. Freeman?"

"Last time I saw her, she was heading to research Lab 3, sir," he reports smartly.

"Good. Carry on."

General Smith waves his arm over the SATCOM's receiver, and the embedded chip in his wrist initiates the encrypted call. "Didn't I tell you never to call me here?"

A harsh digitized voice is heard over the speaker, "We were getting concerned."

"You will have what we agreed on when the time comes, not a moment before."

"I hope you haven't forgotten what's at stake."

"Don't worry. There's a debt to be paid, and I intend to collect it." Adelay strokes the scar on his face. A haunting reminder of what was taken from him by those he trusted the most.

"And the major?"

"Our newly appointed wing commander doesn't have a clue. What a fool. He thinks he's single-handedly saving the world. When I complete the last mission tonight, you can have him."

"Let's hope so, for your sake."

"You should know by now I don't take kindly to threats. Remember what resources I have at my disposal." He glances down at the Devastators, their menacing forms visible below.

"Just make sure it gets done."

Adelay abruptly ends the call, his face a mixture of determination and cold resolve.

LATER THAT NIGHT, Adelay strides alone through the vast expanse of the immense facility. The sound of his footsteps reverberates in the cavernous hangar, creating an eerie ambiance that contrasts with the silence. Overhead, the dim lights cast long, distorted shadows, adding to the sense of solitude. The general steps into the Devastator's command and control center, the pristine white war room accentuated by the ethereal blue glow of the neurotransmitters standing tall in the center.

"Have you jacked in yet?" Adelay checks.

"Any minute now, sir," responds Captain Donahue, the neuroscience officer.

On the center screen is an unsuspecting Tony asleep in his room.

"I want this to go by the numbers. Just like the last two times."

"Yes, sir," confirms Major Barrett, the veteran of over a hundred covert missions.

Tony's brain waves pulse rhythmically across the screen. A display shows "Delta Wave Synchronization Complete."

"Sir, we have a lock," Donahue affirms as he locks in the signal.

The heads-up display for Zeus materializes on the main screen.

"We're in," Barrett announces.

"Good work. Follow the mission profile to the letter. We only have one shot at this."

***

DR. ADRIANNE FREEMAN WORKS FEVERISHLY. A brilliant African-American M.I.T. scientist whose groundbreaking work is responsible for the advances in neuroscience that makes the mind-to-machine connection possible. Her stunning beauty pales in comparison to her intellect. A red light flashes on a console. She checks the clock and calls her assistant.

"John, are there any missions on the schedule for tonight?" she asks.

"No, Dr. Freeman. None that I'm aware of."

"Thanks."

On-screen, Tony becomes restless. A display shows his heart rate and breathing dramatically increasing.

"What's happening?" Adelay asks, tension rising in his voice.

"He's trying to break the lock," Donahue responds.

"But he's sleeping," says Adelay.

"His subconscious is fighting the programming. He's trying to regain control of Zeus."

In his room, Tony begins to sweat heavily. He thrashes violently around the bed. Warning lights flash.

"Delta wave sync is holding, sir, but I don't know how much longer," Donahue warns.

"General, Zeus has acquired the target. Weapon systems are tracking." Barrett is ready to engage.

On the main monitor, the mission specialists can see Zeus' heads-up display, a commercial airliner, and a pair of fighter escorts in his crosshairs. A voice from behind.

"What's going on here?" Adrianne demands.

Adelay is surprised but unfazed.

"I was in the lab and picked up some unusual neural activity. Are there unscheduled tests tonight?" she presses.

"Just some routine simulations, doctor," Adelay coolly responds.

Adrianne sees Tony struggling on-screen.

"These are not simulations! What are you doing to him?" she demands.

"This is a military operation, doctor. I'm going to have to ask you to leave."

As he attempts to escort her out, she evades his grasp.

"So, this is why you've been pushing to alter the transmitting frequencies and change the base programming."

Adelay grabs Adrianne's arm and forces her into the hallway and down the corridor to her lab. He pushes Adrianne roughly into the lab.

"We don't need your permission to conduct tactical operations. You're to deliver the optimized code as planned. Your involvement with this program has come to an end."

"My involvement? This goes beyond the research. You've directly accessed Tony's mind. You can even alter or implant memories. This is unethical, maybe even illegal. I'm completely committed to doing whatever is necessary to ensure the success of this program . . . "

"Are you? Are you really?" he asks. "Everything has a cost, Adrianne. Often a hidden value. Did you really think that there wouldn't be sacrifices, compromises that would be asked of you?"

"Yes, I did. But I didn't know that Tony would be mind-raped and used as a human guinea pig!"

Adelay pulls her close. "You will do as I say!" he commands with a raised voice. "If you care about Tony, you will ensure that this is done. Discreetly, quietly."

She wrenches herself away from Adelay.

"I know your history. You couldn't live with yourself if something happened to him."

"Is that a threat?"

"No. It's a promise."

He's deadly serious.

She turns and walks to her desk. A picture of the research team looks back at her with Tony standing by her side. "You're leaving me no choice."

"I'm glad you finally realize that."

The general leaves the lab and is picked up by his armed escort as he passes through the sliding glass doors. Adrianne remains in the center of her creation, wondering, like Dr. Frankenstein, what monsters she has unleashed upon the world.

LATER THAT NIGHT, Tony steps through the doors of the research laboratory.

"Can I help you, major?" Lieutenant Cummings asks, surprised to see him. He checks his watch. "You're up kind of late, aren't you?"

"Yeah, I couldn't sleep. Have you seen Dr. Freeman?"

"Yes, she's by the neuro-scanner," Lieutenant Cummings replies, grabbing his laptop. "I'm heading out. Good hunting tomorrow."

"Thanks."

Tony quietly enters the lab to find Adrianne, her athletic figure accentuated by her form-fitting jumpsuit, engrossed in her work at a microscope.

"Hello, Dr. Freeman," Tony says softly.

A look of pleasant surprise crosses her face. "Hey, Tony." She glances at her watch. "Wow, you're up late. Couldn't sleep?"

"Yeah, had another one of those incubus nightmares. Some kind of ghost or aberration chasing me. I was hoping you could give me something."

"Well, I would prefer if you'd gotten some natural sleep."

"They're bad."

"Ok," she concedes, walking over to the medicine cabinet. Tony sits in her chair and looks at the screens of her workstation.

"What are you working on?"

She taps out two Valiums in his hand. "I was refining the psychological templates for the Devastators."

On the screen, Tony can see the names of the drones: Zeus, Apollo, and Athena.

"So, why the names of Greek gods?"

She seductively steps behind him, placing her hand over his as she guides the mouse. "I've always loved the archetypes in Greek mythology."

Images of the Greek gods are sequentially displayed on the screen. "The artificial intelligence of the Devastators requires a psychological foundation to be imprinted onto their neural networks. I needed a personality type that was both powerful and omnipotent, as well as having a sense of humanity."

"Well, if I remember correctly, the Greek gods weren't a particularly balanced group of beings. I mean, didn't Cronus eat his own children?"

"Yes! The father of Zeus. The gods are perfect and flawed at the same time. They reflect our strengths in their immortality and our failings in their humanity."

Tony notices a ring on her right hand. He touches it lightly.

"That's beautiful."

The light reflects brilliantly off of the embedded diamonds and fire opal.

"It was an engagement ring."

"Was?"

"He died . . . in a training accident."

"I'm sorry."

"Don't be. It was years ago."

A tear flows down her cheek from the painful memory. "We were just getting to know each other. I didn't even have a chance to tell my family."

She turns Tony in the chair and places her arms around his neck. She leans forward and kisses him passionately.

"Adrianne . . . I don't think this is a good idea."

"But why? I know you feel it too. Why are you fighting what feels so right?"

"I'm heading home to my family in a few days, and despite this attraction I have toward you, I have nothing to offer . . . except heartbreak."

She runs her hand through his hair. "I've always admired your strength, your power—qualities so few men have."

She points to a picture on the wall of an epic battle. "You're like Perseus, the destroyer of evil."

Tony stands and gazes at her perfect features. Her chestnut complexion, her beautiful golden-brown eyes. "If I'm Perseus, that would make you Athena; she forged the weapons he used to behead Medusa."

"I guess you're right."

"I'm going to head out. It's a big day tomorrow."

"Don't you wish you could take back things you've done? To make a clean start?"

"All the time," Tony admits.

"I would escape to a desert island if I could right now . . . warm breeze on my face . . . sand beneath my feet."

"We all have regrets about our past. It's how we learn from them that defines who we are." She reaches out and touches his face. "You have such a good heart, Tony. Promise me you'll watch your back."

"Isn't that what I have you for?"

The inexplicable attraction between them overwhelms him. He lifts her off her feet and kisses her. Their arms and legs entwined in a passionate embrace. The lab, filled with the hum of machines and the glow of monitors, is transformed into a world of its own, where time stands still, and the outside world ceases to exist.

Their passion ignites, and their love, fueled by the intensity of their attraction, takes them on a journey of exploration and tenderness. They discover each other's bodies, their hands tracing every contour, their lips tasting every inch of skin. They share their deepest desires and fears and, in that moment, they become more than lovers; they become one. They know that their connection goes beyond the physical. The world outside the lab may be uncertain and dangerous, but in each other's arms, they find a refuge from the storm that awaits them.

CHAPTER 3
BLACKOUT

TONY CONFIDENTLY STRIDES through the labyrinthine halls of the state-of-the-art research complex. As he approaches the reinforced steel doors of the command center, Tony submits to a series of advanced biometric scans. The fluorescent lights above flicker, casting an eerie glow on the sterile white walls. Each step he takes echoes with the surefooted confidence of a seasoned fighter pilot. Salutes snap crisply in his direction, and he returns them with equal precision. The doors part with a hiss, granting him access to the Devastator 5 control center. The atmosphere inside is electric, charged with the anticipation of the mission ahead.

Adrianne greets him with a warm smile, her eyes shining as she hands him the mission checklist, her voice steady and professional, "Morning, major."

"Morning, doctor."

"Did you sleep well?" she asks, her tone teasing.

Tony glances up from the clipboard, the corner of his mouth lifting in a wry grin. "No, thanks to you."

Adrianne feigns innocence, her smile widening. "Oh, I forgot to congratulate you on your appointment."

"That's right, you didn't," Tony retorts, his eyes still on the checklist.

"Considering you're the only person in the world who can control the Devastators, it must have been a tough decision," she muses, a note of admiration in her voice.

Tony looks up, his grin turning cocky. "Don't worry, when I receive the Nobel Peace Prize for ridding the world of terrorism, I'll be sure to mention your name."

He deftly blocks her playful slap. "You better," she warns.

Tony hands her back the checklist and addresses the Devastator 5 mission specialist, a man hunching over a console, his fingers flying over the keyboard. "Status?" he asks, his voice all business.

"The Uzbek rebel leader, Dilshod Nabiev, is still en route to a meeting with the Iranian defense minister," the specialist replies, his voice tense.

"Excellent," Tony declares, the excitement in his voice barely contained. "We can stop a major uprising and mess with the Iranians all before lunch."

"A fitting end to the research, don't you think?" Adrianne inquires, her gaze fixed on the displays of her medical console.

Tony takes a seat in the commander's chair, which hovers in the center of the control room. "I'm just getting warmed up, doctor. The Russians and Chinese are up next. They're going to get a much-needed reminder of who wears the pants on this side of the globe."

"Alright, let's wake them up," he commands, his voice low and steady.

Taking two deep breaths, Tony settles himself and transmits a systems startup order. His eyes glaze over in a bluish haze, a direct connection to the drones established. "This is Cronus, initiate start sequence. Prepare for reentry. Upload mission profile Z1304. Respond."

"Acknowledged. Activating guidance systems. Preparing for Earth reentry," Zeus, Apollo, and Athena answer in unison.

In Tony's mind, the system readouts and video displays of the three drones materialize in a virtual space, providing him with a seamless interface to control them.

High above the Earth's surface, the Devastators retract their solar panels and assume a diamond formation. Zeus takes the lead position, its dark, angular hull cutting through the thin atmosphere like a knife.

"On my mark, initiate reentry in 3 . . . 2 . . . 1 . . . GO!"

The Devastators fire their powerful fusion engines, performing a perfect barrel roll as they rocket earthward. The triple sonic booms of their reentry create rippled concussive waves, blasting away surrounding cloud cover.

"Sir, the Devastators have reentered the atmosphere and are currently vectored to the mission area. Terminal velocity is Mach 25," the specialist reports. "Targets are on the move."

"Roger that. Initiating stealth systems," Tony responds, his voice calm and authoritative.

In suborbital space, the Devastators shimmer and shift as their nanotechnology changes their surface, rendering them invisible. "Blackout," Tony commands.

"Acknowledged," Zeus, Apollo, and Athena reply in unison.

Back at the command center, "Sir, the Devastators have fallen off radar. They have no residual electronic signature."

Adrianne monitors Tony's vitals, her eyes flicking between the screens displaying his biometric data. A display spikes into the red. "Tony, I'm reading elevated cortisol levels in your system," she says, concern creeping into her voice.

"I'm fine," Tony reassures her, focusing on the mission. "Now, if you don't mind, I have some bad guys to dispose of."

The Devastators scan the terrain and identify a group of vehicles winding their way through the mountains.

"Major, the target has entered the mission area. Intercept in 90 seconds."

"Roger that. Plenty of time," Tony replies, his tone cool and collected. He watches as the Devastators hit the coastline at

Mach 4, their powerful engines streaking across the sky. Adrianne notices another spike in Tony's readings, her eyes widening with concern. "Tony, I'm really not liking what I'm reading here."

"Target has just come over the ridge," the mission specialist interrupts.

"I see them," Tony confirms, his voice straining.

Sweat beads on Tony's brow as his heart rate soars. Adrianne's voice trembles as she urges, "Tony, you need to abort the mission! Your heart rate is through the roof!"

"That's not going to happen, doctor!" Tony growls, his grip on the command chair tightening.

The Devastators tighten their formation as they approach their unsuspecting prey. "Activate weapons systems. Attack formation Sierra," Tony commands, his voice still straining.

"Acknowledged," Zeus, Apollo, and Athena respond.

Apollo jams all outgoing communications while Athena scans the sky for potential air threats. Zeus opens its weapons bay, revealing a massive ion cannon. It glows red and orange as it prepares to fire.

"Tony, shut it down! It's too dangerous!" Adrianne implores, her eyes wide with fear.

"No! I got this!" Tony insists, his knuckles white as he clenches the armrests of his chair.

As she grabs his shoulder, he stands and faces her with craziness in his eyes. Flashes of light blind him as a series of disjointed images assault his mind . . .

— A crying newborn.
— A sandy beach with turquoise seas.
— Bloody feet leaving bloody footprints on a white floor.
— A young boy with blond hair screams, "Help me, Tony!"
— A dark ghost-like figure walks through a bright open doorway.
— An arid desert, a sweltering jungle, a cloudless blue sky.
— Water defies gravity and runs up a moldy, slimy wall.
— Hundreds of rats run over a child's bed.
— A series of bright strobing lights.
— Young bloody hands.

Suddenly, Tony finds himself standing, his hand gripping Adrianne's collar, his fist drawn back. The assembled team rushes to her aid.

"Tony! Tony!" Adrianne cries out.

He shakes himself lucid and releases his grip on Adrianne.

"Major! The mission!"

"Abort! Abort! Abort!" Tony commands, his voice hoarse and weak.

High above the rugged landscape of northern Iran, Zeus retracts its ion cannon. "Reassume ready position 4," Tony orders, his voice barely audible.

"Acknowledged," Zeus, Apollo, and Athena respond in unison. The Devastators pass silently over their intended targets and rocket back into suborbital space.

Tony collapses into his chair, sweat pouring down his face as his hands shake uncontrollably. "Tony? Tony? Can you hear me?" Adrianne asks, her voice shaking.

"Yeah . . . My head is killing me," Tony manages to gasp, his breathing labored.

Turning to a nearby tech, "Help me get him to the medical unit," Adrianne orders.

"What happened? Tell me what's wrong. It's so familiar. It all seems so familiar," Tony mutters, his eyes unfocused and dazed.

"You had a brainstorm. Your MEG and EEG readings were

off the chart. We need to get you over to the medbay. Don't worry, you're going to be alright, I won't let anything happen to you." Her eyes fill with determination as she squeezes his hand. "I promise."

HIGH ABOVE THE EARTH, the Devastators resume their silent vigil in suborbital space. Like ancient sentinels standing guard, they resume their overwatch.

CHAPTER 4

THE UNITED STATES OF CHINA

IN THE SHADOW of a sprawling warehouse, a sleek, black 18-wheeler sits concealed among a fleet of unassuming Mercedes panel vans. Miniature killer drones, nearly imperceptible to the naked eye, patrol the perimeter with lethal efficiency. Chinese soldiers disguised in common coveralls blend seamlessly with the workers, vigilantly standing guard.

Inside the mobile command center, digital and holographic displays flank either side, manned by a small army of elite commandos dressed in black multicam uniforms. At the heart of the operation, a naked man stands immobile within a glass cylinder filled with swirling yellow and red gas. Holographic displays reveal a human body augmented with a state-of-the-art mechanical exoskeleton and a neural interface at the base of his skull.

Tensions between China and the United States have escalated in recent years, fueled by competing economic interests, territorial disputes in the South China Sea, and an escalating cyberwarfare campaign. The Chinese government, determined to supplant the United States as the dominant global power, has embarked on a daring plan to take control of the US's most powerful weapon: the Devastator 5 combat drones.

Major Fang Xiao, the operation's second-in-command, enters the command center. "Colonel, it's time. The satellite is in position," he announces.

Colonel Zhang Jike's eyes snap open. A formidable figure in the Chinese Army Special Forces, Jike is a veteran of over a dozen covert missions and the embodiment of China's most advanced cybernetic technology. He is a super soldier designed for a singular purpose: the infiltration and subversion of the United States. "Initiate the uplink. I'll be right there," Jike responds.

Jike and Xiao enter the communications van, and a hologram of General Zu-Shan Lee flickers to life. At 67, Lee is the commander of the South Blade special operations unit, a secretive and elite force within the Chinese military.

"Greetings, colonel. What is your report?" Zu-Shan inquires, his gaze piercing and resolute.

"All units are in place and operational, general," Jike replies, his expression unwavering.

"Excellent," Zu-Shan says, a hint of satisfaction in his voice.

"Major Simmons is due to arrive in Washington in two days. Once we take him down, I will make an imprint of his neural net and assume control of the drones. Without their superweapon, they will be unable to stop us," Jike explains, his words measured and precise.

"America will fall as prophesied, general. The birth of the United States of China is all but certain."

A FULL MOON casts stark shadows across the barren landscape surrounding the secret underground facility, its location deep in the high desert of Uzbekistan. The tension in the air is palpable as Tony prepares for a brief moment of connection with his family.

"Is the link up, Dave?" Tony asks, his voice betraying a mix of anticipation and apprehension.

"Yes, sir. I have you set up on station 7. I'm afraid the window's going to be short this time, major," Dave replies.

"Roger that."

Tony sits down in front of a screen filled with static, waiting for his wife, Jennifer, to appear. Tall and blonde, she is the epitome of grace and the perfect mother. He often wonders what she saw in him, but he thanks God every day that she saw enough to say, "I do." The static clears as the satellite swings into position.

"Hello? Hello, can you hear me? Tony?"

"Hey Babe! I can hear you."

"Oh, sweetheart, it's so great to hear your voice."

"How are you?"

"Better now that I'm talking to you," a smile dancing on her lips.

"I know. It's almost over. Just a few more days."

"God, I can't wait to see you," Jennifer admits, her eyes glistening with unshed tears.

"Where are the kids?" Tony asks, eager to hear their voices.

"They were in karate class. They just pulled in," Jennifer explains, the sound of the front door opening punctuating her words. The front door bursts open as the kids rush in, followed by a family friend, Jim.

"Dad!" they scream in unison, their excitement palpable.

"Hey! How are my little warriors?" Tony asks, his voice filled with pride.

They speak at once.

"OK, wait a minute!" Jennifer interrupts. A temporary calm ensues. "I want you guys to go upstairs and put your gear away, and then you can talk to your dad. You better hurry because he doesn't have much time."

They rocket out of the room, each one hoping to be the first one back. Jim steps into view. "Tony, you remember Jim?"

"Of course I do. He still has my circular saw."

"Oh, right. I'll be sure to get that back to you when you get home."

"No worries," Tony says, dismissing the matter with a wave of his hand.

"Jim is in my combat jiujitsu class. Hey! We learned about disarming a gunman yesterday. Let me show you!" She hands Jim a wooden spoon from the kitchen drawer.

"Jim, you stand here. Now just like in class." Her enthusiasm is infectious.

"You got it," Jim agrees, stepping into position.

Jim raises the deadly spoon to Jennifer's head. With lightning speed, she grabs Jim's wrist and holds on tightly as she twists it expertly, forcing Jim down on one knee. In her excitement, she turns Jim's wrist over too far, sending him flying across the kitchen floor and onto his back right in front of Matthew.

"Finish him!"

"Oh my God, Jim! I'm so sorry!" Jennifer exclaims, her face flushed with embarrassment.

"Ouch! That's gotta hurt," Tony sympathizes, wincing in solidarity.

"Mom! You have to finish him!"

Jim gets up slowly, rubbing his back gingerly. "I'm OK. I'd say you got that move down."

"Jim, I'm so sorry, I had no idea . . ." Jennifer trails off, her voice laden with regret.

"Really, I'm fine, but I'm definitely going to leave before the next demonstration."

Masking the pain, Jim grabs his jacket on the way out. "Safe home, Tony. I'll be sure to have your saw ready. I don't want you to send Jennifer to come for it."

With the show over, the kids rush to the holographic display. "Okay! Where are my little lions?" Tony asks, eager to engage with his children.

The twins, Amanda and Brittany, both 12 years old and

wearing matching nightgowns, greet their father. "We still watch the movie you got us before you left," Amanda says, her voice tinged with nostalgia.

"*The Lion King*? Aren't you guys getting a little tired of it by now?" Tony asks.

"No! It's perfect. It reminds us of you. We watch it every day!" Brittany exclaims.

"And I really want to thank you for that, honey," Jennifer says sarcastically.

"We learned the words to 'Hakuna Matata' and sing it with a Jenny Blaze backbeat," Amanda boasts, her face lighting up with excitement.

"Jenny who?" Tony asks, puzzled.

"Don't ask," Jennifer warns, shaking her head.

"And we're really good! Listen . . ." Brittany begins, as she and her sister start a dance routine a little too provocative for their age.

"Wow, OK . . . You guys are so good. I think you should watch *The Lion King* three times a day."

Jennifer shakes her fist from across the room. "Remember what I'm capable of," she warns, a playful glint in her eye.

"Good point," Tony concedes, chuckling.

Tony can see that Matthew, his youngest child, is quieter than usual. "Hey, champ, how's it going?" he asks, concern etched on his face.

"OK," Matthew mumbles, his eyes downcast.

There's something wrong. "Hey, girls, can you give your brother and me a minute?" Tony asks, seeking some privacy for his conversation with Matthew.

"It's time for bed anyway. Say good night to your father," Jennifer instructs the girls, ushering them toward the stairs.

"Good night!" Amanda and Brittany chime in unison.

"Sleep tight, sweethearts. I'll see you soon. Love you!" Tony calls after them, his voice soft and full of love.

"Love you too!" the girls reply, their voices echoing down the stairwell.

Jennifer ushers the girls upstairs, leaving Tony and Matthew alone.

"So tell me, champ, what's going on?" Tony inquires, his brow furrowed in concern.

"Amanda and Brittany said I'm weak," Matthew explains, his voice cracking with emotion.

"What? Why?" Tony asks, his eyes narrowing with concern.

"They said that the female lions are the ones that do all of the hunting, and that the male lion is lazy and useless," Matthew reveals, his face downcast.

"I see," Tony murmurs, understanding dawning on his face.

"You said that the male lion was the mightiest of all the animals and king of the jungle."

"Well, he is," Tony reassures his son, his voice firm and confident. "The male lion lets the female lion do all of the hunting for him while he gets to lay around all day in the shade."

"Really?" Matthew's eyes widen with curiosity and surprise.

"Yes! He's the first to eat, and he can do anything he wants," Tony continues, hoping to restore his son's confidence.

"That's so cool!" Matthew exclaims, his spirits visibly lifted.

Jennifer returns to the kitchen, having overheard part of the conversation. "Hey, Mom! Dad said I didn't have to go to school or do any chores! And that you have to feed me whatever I want!" Matthew proclaims, a cheeky grin on his face.

"Oh, really?" Jennifer raises an eyebrow and turns to Tony, seeking clarification.

"I didn't say that . . . exactly," Tony admits, a sheepish smile creeping onto his face.

"Honey, go up to bed. I'll be there in a minute," Jennifer instructs Matthew, her tone firm but gentle.

"I swear I didn't say that. I was just trying to help," Tony insists, his hands raised in surrender.

"You want to help? Then don't help!" Jennifer teases, laughter bubbling up from within. They both laugh, their eyes locked in a moment of shared amusement. Static begins to build on the screen, signaling the end of their brief connection.

"Sorry, major, the window is closing," Dave explains, his voice apologetic.

"Sweetheart, the satellite is moving out of position," Tony informs Jennifer, his voice heavy with regret.

"I miss you so much," Jennifer whispers, her eyes glistening with tears.

"I miss you too," Tony replies, his heart aching with longing.

"It's been so hard going to sleep each night without you by my side. To hold me, to whisper in my ear that everything will be alright," Jennifer confesses, her voice trembling with emotion.

"It will be. I promise when I get back, let's go up to the mountains and see your mom like we used to," Tony suggests, his voice filled with warmth and hope.

The picture begins to fade. "I have to go. I love you," Tony says, his voice thick with emotion.

"I love you t . . ." Jennifer's voice is cut off as the screen goes blank. White noise fills the room. Tony touches the empty screen, his hand lingering for a moment before he gets up abruptly to leave.

"Thanks, Dave," Tony says, his voice barely audible.

"No problem, major," Dave replies, his face a mask of sympathy as he watches Tony walk away, back to the lonely, dangerous world that lies beyond the horizon.

CHAPTER 5
TWO HEARTS

THE ATMOSPHERE BUZZES with energy as members of the Devastator 5 team revel in the successful completion of their research. Party hats adorn their heads, and the pulsating music reverberates through the hangar. Adrianne spots Tony standing by the hangar doors, his gaze fixed on the star-studded night sky.

"Making a wish?" Adrianne inquires, her voice curious and teasing.

"Sort of," Tony replies, his mind seemingly elsewhere.

The moon casts a gentle glow on Adrianne's raven hair as she approaches him. "What are you doing standing here all alone? The party is over there." She gestures toward the raucous celebration, her eyes sparkling with amusement.

"Yeah, I know. I have a lot on my mind," Tony admits, his voice tinged with a hint of melancholy. Adrianne moves in close, taking his hand as her breasts gently brush across his chest.

"Well, maybe there's something I can do to take your mind off of things."

"Addy, don't . . ." Tony warns, his voice strained.

"Don't what?" she challenges, her voice sultry and provocative. Pressing herself against him, she sways her hips to the rhythm of the music, her movements sensual and enticing. "Adrianne, this can't happen again. I'm sorry, it just can't," Tony insists, his voice firm yet gentle.

Unfazed, Adrianne wraps her arms around his waist, resting her head on his chest. She listens intently to his pounding heartbeat. "Are you sure? Your heart says 'yes.'"

Tony carefully pushes her back, his eyes filled with a mixture of longing and regret. "Then you're not listening closely enough. I have this strong connection to you that I don't understand—as if I know you from a past life. But what we shared is over. It can't happen again. I love my wife. I realize that now more than ever."

"Come on, baby, let me feel you again," Adrianne pleads, desperation lacing her voice.

"I'm serious," Tony asserts, his expression resolute.

Adrianne pulls away, struggling to hold back her tears. "So what was it then? A fling? An interlude? A romance?"

"A mistake," Tony confesses, the words slicing through the tense silence like a razor-sharp blade.

"I loved you . . . I love you," Adrianne admits, her voice cracking with emotion.

"I know . . . I hoped you'd understand," Tony says, his tone somber and apologetic.

"Understand what? That the most amazing man I have ever known is walking out of my life forever? I'm postdoctoral at M.I.T. I understand a lot of things, Tony, but this is not one of them." Her voice trembles as she takes his hand and places it on her heart, "Tony, we're good together. You touched my heart and soul in ways I didn't think were possible. We were one."

Tony slowly withdraws his hand, his eyes glistening with unshed tears. "I felt it too, but that time is over. I'm sorry." He turns and walks away, leaving Adrianne standing in the middle of the hangar.

"So that's it? Just like that? Wham, bam, thank you, ma'am?" she calls out, her voice filled with anger and despair. The partygoers part like the Red Sea as Tony makes his way through the crowd.

"You don't get to say when it's over, Tony! I do!" Adrianne yells, her voice cracking with heartache. Everyone falls silent, their eyes riveted on the unfolding scene. The door closes slowly behind Tony, its finality echoing through the hangar.

"You don't say when it's over, I do!" Adrianne repeats, her voice raw with emotion. Left standing alone amidst the vast expanse of the hangar, Adrianne's words ricochet off the walls, reverberating into the night. The partygoers exchange uneasy glances, unsure of how to proceed. The atmosphere, once electric with celebration, now feels heavy with the weight of heartache and loss.

Adrianne's breathing comes in ragged gasps as she attempts to regain her composure. The music, once lively and boisterous, now feels like a cruel mockery of her pain. She turns away from the curious onlookers, her shoulders shaking with the effort to hold back her tears.

Meanwhile, Tony strides purposefully away from the party, his heart aching with the knowledge of the pain he's caused. He knows he's made the right decision, but it doesn't make the sting of loss any easier to bear.

As the door to the hangar closes behind him, he takes a deep breath, his thoughts racing. He knows that the decision he's made is not only for himself but for his family and the life he's built with them. The memory of his wife and children, their laughter and love, bolsters his resolve as he walks away from the past.

CHAPTER 6
INTERCEPT

ANDREWS AFB, VIRGINIA

THE C-17 GLOBEMASTER III, a military transport aircraft, touches down with a roar, decelerating as it taxis to a stop near a line of black SUVs and armored tactical vehicles. The research team, accompanied by Tony, Adrianne, and Adelay, disembarks and swiftly boards the waiting convoy. Two armed Airborne Rangers flank the trio as they climb into an SUV.

ON A BUSY STREET, four unmarked black vans streak through traffic. Inside the lead vehicle, Colonel Jike and his team track the convoy's progress on a holographic heads-up display (HUD) projected above the dashboard. Xiao, Jike's second-in-command, points at the map. "We can intercept them here," Xiao says, noting the limited escape options once the convoy crosses the river. Jike nods in agreement, and the strike team accelerates, weaving recklessly through the congestion.

THE CONVOY THUNDERS DOWN I-495, escorted by a phalanx of police vehicles that clear a path ahead. As they proceed, tension mounts inside the SUV. Adelay pulls out a folder and questions the others about the last operation. "I've read the post-action report on the Iranian mission, doctor. What happened?" Adelay demands.

"It was an anomaly. Nothing to be concerned about. Tony's fine," Adrianne reassures him.

Adelay, unsatisfied, presses further, "If there's a problem, I need to know. Major?"

Tony looks at Adrianne, weighing his words carefully, "Adrianne, he needs to know."

"Tony, don't . . ." Adrianne's voice is tinged with caution.

"Know what?" Adelay's patience is wearing thin.

JIKE'S TEAM reaches the ambush site. Working quickly, they anchor a massive railgun to the pavement. Suddenly, one of the supports snaps, sending the 1,000-pounds weapon crashing to the ground. Jike races over then heaves the railgun onto his shoulder with a grunt. His augmented frame easily carries the weight. He aims it at the oncoming traffic, tracking the convoy as it speeds into view. The railgun locks onto its target . . .

TONY OPENS UP TO ADELAY, "I've been having nightmares. Night sweats, the works." Adelay's gaze shifts to Adrianne.

"It's nothing to worry about. We have it under control," Adrianne answers nervously.

"I doubt that. I warned you, doctor. If you didn't handle this, I would . . ."

Suddenly, a deep bass vibration rocks the SUV. A blue flash streaks by as the railgun fires a tungsten slug at near lightspeed and strikes the SUV head-on, knocking the engine completely from the compartment and sending the vehicle high into the air. The obliterated vehicle tumbles end over end, lands on its top, then slides to a halt.

Smoke and debris are strewn across the highway. Cut and bruised, Tony climbs out of the inverted vehicle only to find Adelay and Adrianne dead.

A vision of her passes through his mind . . .

Adrianne smiles as she lies next to him in bed under bright white billowing sheets.

He looks around, disoriented, and sees Jike approaching through the smoke. Gunfire erupts as the convoy's escort engages the assailants. Tony snatches a firearm from a fallen ranger and takes cover behind an armored transport, where he finds the escort's commander barking orders.

"Sierra team, move to a flanking position and engage!" the commander yells.

"What's happening? Who's attacking us?" Tony shouts over the chaos.

"Unknown. Multiple attackers are advancing up the highway. They must have known our route. Backup is inbound, ETA 10 minutes. You're the target, Major. We need to...," the commander replies, only to be cut off as a bullet slices through his throat, spraying blood across Tony and the vehicle.

Tony catches the commander's limp body, watching the life leave his eyes. More bullets strike the armor just above his head, and he knows he has to move . . . now! He crosses the highway and dodges traffic in the oncoming lanes as he looks for safety.

In the distance, he watches Jike lift a soldier off his feet with one arm and fling him through an SUV. Tony jumps a barrier and falls hard on the street meters below. Scrambling to his feet, he disappears into the city's busy streets.

While running, Tony becomes dizzy. He stumbles onto his hands and knees, sweating, heart racing, then passes out . . .

An arid and barren desert passes below at incredible speed. A shapeless, morphing black figure appears, following the terrain with amazing agility. Ahead a military convoy is racing across the desert as if running for its life. Sensing the fear, it dives as a falcon would to intercept its prey. Hardened armored vehicles, filled with weapons and supplies, explode in violent clusters as the apparition passes overhead. A metallic voice screams in his head . . .
"We Are One!"

As Tony regains consciousness, he finds himself surrounded by strangers on the busy city street. Struggling to his feet, he notices people snapping photos of him with their cell phones. He pushes through the crowd, staggering away.

A UPS truck stops nearby to make a delivery. As the driver steps out, Tony seizes the opportunity, jumping into the driver's seat and speeding off, narrowly avoiding an oncoming police car with sirens wailing. He has to get home.

When Tony reaches his house, he leaps out of the still-moving delivery truck as it smashes into the mailbox. He runs across the lawn, but the front door is locked. Drawing his weapon, he kicks the door open. "Jennifer . . .! Matthew . . .! Amanda . . .! Brittany . . .!" he shouts, frantic, tearing the house apart in search of his family.

His worst fears are realized when he discovers they're gone. Rushing back outside, Tony spots his neighbor, Jim, entering his home across the street. "Hey, Jim! Jim! It's me, Tony!"

Jim turns. "Hey, Tony . . ."

The sharp crack of a sniper rifle cuts through the air, and a bullet strikes Jim between the eyes, killing him instantly. A second round hits Tony in his shoulder, sending him tumbling down a small embankment. He struggles to his feet and takes cover behind a cluster of trees across the road. Peering through the bushes, Tony sees Jike leading a group of soldiers up the street.

As they approach, Tony bursts out from cover and fires two rounds, hitting Jike squarely in the chest. Jike winces and then smiles back at Tony.

"Holy shit! What the . . ." Tony ducks to avoid the barrage of incoming gunfire and makes a run for it.

He reaches the main road, pulls a belligerent driver from a passing car, and speeds away. Shots ring out, shattering the back window. Lighting up the rear tires, he creates a smoke screen and escapes. Tony weaves desperately in and out of traffic. Blood soaking the car seat . . .

Tony and Matthew play catch during a camping trip while Jennifer, Brittany, and Amanda fix lunch.

He loses consciousness and crashes into a bus stop. Bystanders come to Tony's aid and call 911.

JANICE, Rasheed, and Sam are finishing their break at a local drive-thru when their dispatcher's voice comes through the radio.

"EM-223, EM-223, single car accident, corner of Wabash and Lake. Respond."

"C'mon guys, let's roll," Janice says. Unbeknownst to them, one of Jike's team intercepts the 911 call and moves to the scene in their relentless pursuit of Tony.

CHAPTER 7
CHASING SHADOWS

PRESENT TIME

THE AMBULANCE CREW, powerless to help, watches Tony, battered and bleeding profusely, disappear down a pitch-black alley.

IN THE COMMAND VEHICLE, Jike and Xaio lose communication with the van pursuing the ambulance. Xaio keys the mic several times, but only static comes through. "No response from Unit 4, Colonel."

Jike's unwavering focus remains on the task at hand, and he grips the steel door handle so hard that it bends. "We must find Simmons. The fate of China depends on it."

TONY SCRAMBLES OVER A FENCE, landing heavily on the rain-soaked ground. A dog barks in the distance. He drags himself across the yard of a two-story house - the only one with power in a neighborhood shrouded in darkness. Suddenly, the area is flooded with light, and the deafening boom of a shotgun fills the air.

"Wow, that was loud!" exclaims the man with the shotgun, wiggling his finger in his ear. "Who goes there? Don't make me shoot you! I will, but only if I have to, so don't make me have to, or we'll both be sorry, but more you than me."

Weak from blood loss, Tony manages to say, "Spencer . . . it's me . . . " Recognizing his old friend, Spencer lowers the shotgun and rushes to Tony's side.

"My God, Tony?" He notices Tony's gunshot wound. "You've been shot! Let's get you inside."

Spencer drags Tony into the house and down a narrow passageway leading to the basement. The room is a model of organization, filled with meticulously arranged shelves of electronic equipment and inventions.

As Spencer lays Tony down on a nearby table, Tony murmurs in a delirious state, "They're gone . . . they're gone . . . "

"Who's gone?" Spencer asks, concerned.

"My family . . . they're gone . . . they took my family"

Spencer examines the gunshot wound under Tony's jumpsuit and bandages. "Oh, this is bad. I'll have to stitch you up. Hold on! Stay with me, Tony! Stay with me!" Rummaging through a closet, Spencer retrieves medical supplies and starts an IV.

"Where are they? I have to get to them, they're in danger . . . You have to help me get them back . . . " Tony loses consciousness as Spencer works feverishly to save his life.

TONY AWAKENS to the sound of Mozart and a large, curious cat on his chest. He tries to sit up, wincing at the pain in his heavily bandaged shoulder. The cat, satisfied with its investigation, jumps down.

"That's Thelonious," Spencer says, introducing his feline companion as he checks the IV.

"Tony Simmons. I can't believe it's you. When was the last time we saw each other? It has to be, what, five, six years ago?"

"Yeah, that's about right."

"You lost a lot of blood last night. If you hadn't gotten here when you did, we'd be having this conversation through a medium."

"Thanks. I owe you one."

"Well, with all that you did for me when they booted me from S.Y.N.C., I'd say we're even."

Spencer picks up a picture of him and Tony in front of a B-2 stealth bomber.

"I know you've had a tough time since the hearing, but you have to know, Spencer, it wasn't your fault."

"Well, no one else saw it that way, especially General Smith."

"Can you blame him? He lost his son on that mission and nearly didn't make it back himself. Deep wounds heal slowly, if at all."

"Well, at least you kept me out of prison." Spencer's gaze turns distant, haunted by memories. "I still have nightmares about that night. So many good people gone . . . cut to ribbons . . . just like that."

"There's no way for you to have known."

Spencer slams his fist against his chest. "You're wrong! I should have known! I should have seen that their stealth suits would fail. It was my responsibility! My job!"

In a fit of frustration, Spencer kicks over a tool rack, scattering tools across the floor. His OCD kicks in as he rushes to pick them up. "1 and 2, 2 and 3, 3 and 4, 4 and 5, one fish, two fish, red fish, blue fish . . ."

"Spencer . . ." Tony approaches Spencer, who is hunched over the disarrayed tools, nervously aligning them.

"The hills are alive . . . ," Spencer blurts out.

Tony bends over and lifts Spencer by the shoulders. "Spencer, look at me."

Spencer clutches the tools to his chest. "The important thing is that you found out why the stealth suits failed, and because of that, you saved the lives of countless others that night. In my eyes, you're a hero. You hear me? A hero."

Spencer smiles weakly. "You're a great friend, Tony."

"And so are you."

Shifting his weight, Tony winces in pain. "Let me get you something to ease the pain. I'm sure I have something illicit around here to give you."

"No, I need to stay clear. I have to find my family." Tony recounts the events of the last 72 hours.

"Oh my God! We need answers. Yes, answers. The who, what, where, when, why, and how. But mostly who."

"I have to reconnect to the Devastators. That's the first priority. Whoever is after me is also looking to take control of them. We have to be first. Once I'm connected, I can use them to find Jen and the kids."

"Well, how are you gonna do that? You just can't waltz into S.Y.N.C. Headquarters and ask, 'Have you seen my invisible drones?'"

"Adrianne is the key. She was the only one who knew the Devastators inside and out."

"But . . ."

"Yeah, I know, she's dead."

Spencer walks over to his vast array of computers and pulls up Adrianne's profile. "Wow. She was an amazing woman."

"Yeah. She was."

"It says here that she had an office in Northwest D.C. Maybe we can find out something about her research there and figure out how to get you reconnected."

"Sounds like a plan. There has to be a way. There just has to be!" Resolved to uncover the truth, Tony and Spencer begin their dangerous journey, knowing that the fate of Tony's family and the Devastators hangs in the balance.

CHAPTER 8
STAY TOGETHER

JENNIFER MANEUVERS the family minivan into the parking lot of the Oasis Banquet Hall, the vehicle's tires crunching on the gravel. They enter the main ballroom to find the festivities well underway. A "Welcome Home" banner arches across the stage, its bold letters illuminated by the warm glow of overhead spotlights.

The event coordinator, Barbara Collins, 28, tall and impeccably dressed, her designer glasses perfectly matching her accessories, greets the Simmons family with a warm smile," "Mrs. Simmons?"

"Yes. I'm sorry we're late. This is all so last minute. We got here as fast as we can," Jennifer replies, a hint of nervousness in her voice.

"Oh, it's no problem, we were just getting started. The research team is here already. We were just waiting for Tony and the others to arrive."

"It's so nice of you to organize all of this."

"It's the least that the Defense Department can do. We know how hard these long deployments can be on the families."

Matthew and the girls spot several friends across the room. "Hey, Mom, Aaron's here!"

"Okay. Don't go too far. Your dad should be here soon."

Matthew joins the group of boys. From the corner of his eye, he spies two men wheeling a large container into the kitchen. "Hey, did you see that?"

"See what?," Arron asks.

"Those guys were bringing in huge boxes."

"What do you think is in them? Strippers?"

"I don't know, let's check it out."

The two boys stealthily move along the wall to the kitchen doors and peek around the corner. As they see the two men leave, the boys sneak into the kitchen and hide behind a stainless steel refrigerator. On the counters, they spot dozens of long black bags with zippers.

"What do you think is in the bags?"

"I don't know."

"We should look," Aaron dares.

"No way!"

"C'mon! Don't be chicken."

Aaron cautiously approaches the nearest bag and begins to unzip it . . . The door slams open as the men return with another container. The boys duck out of sight. The men open the container and remove three more black bags, then leave.

Matthew decides he's seen enough. "Come on, let's get out of here."

"I want to see what's in the bags."

Aaron slowly unzips one . . . he screams . . . a dead boy stares back at him. They sprint back into the main ballroom.

"Mom!"

Jennifer turns to see her terrified son running toward her. Masked men wielding submachine guns burst into the hall. They begin grabbing the families and forcing them to the floor.

"Everyone down! Do it now!" the leader demands.

"Mom, I'm scared," whispers Brittany.

Jennifer grabs the leader as he passes. "What's going on?"

"There's been an incident. We are moving you to a secure location. Please go outside and get on the bus!"

Through the glass side doors, Jennifer can see several buses parked just outside the hall. Fearing for her family's safety, she gathers them together and boards an awaiting bus.

The commando leader pulls Barbara aside. "The convoy was attacked. We have to accelerate our plans."

"We need Major Simmons."

"There's no time."

"Then take the bodies out of the kitchen and place them near the back exit. I'll handle the police and media when they arrive."

The gunmen remove the bodies from the black bags and place them near the rear of the building. One for each member of the research team. The gas lines from the ovens are cut. A bomb on a digital timer starts a 60-second countdown.

"Move! Move! Move!"

The bus pulls away at high speed. Moments later, a thunderous explosion rocks the bus as the catering hall is engulfed in flames. Jennifer shields her children from the blast, and she feels the heat from the fireball on her back. She grabs one of the commandos standing by the door.

"What was that explosion? What the hell is going on?" she demands.

"Sit down and shut up!" He slightly raises his rifle as a warning. Jennifer stares at him in an intense face-off, then slowly sits down. Turning slowly, he moves to the front of the bus.

"Mom, who are these men? Where are they taking us?"

Unsure of what's happening, she answers to reassure her kids, "They're taking us to a safe place, honey."

"Mom, Aaron and I saw a bunch of black bags in the kitchen. They had bodies in them."

"What? Bodies? Are you sure?"

"We saw them! I swear!"

Jennifer looks at the heavily armed men sitting strategically around the cabin. "Stay close to me. No matter what happens, we stay together. Understood?"

The kids nod. Sirens can be heard approaching in the distance. Several police cars pass the buses in the opposite direction, heading toward the raging inferno.

As the bus barrels down the road, Jennifer tries to remain calm for her children, her mind racing with questions. The armed men surrounding them, their identities hidden by masks, offer no reassurance. Jennifer glances out the window, noticing the landscape becoming more desolate as they leave the city limits.

The bus finally comes to a halt in front of a nondescript warehouse. The commandos escort the families inside, their boots echoing off the concrete floor. Jennifer clutches her children close, trying to offer comfort in the face of the unknown.

Inside the warehouse, the families find themselves in a makeshift command center filled with monitors and advanced communication equipment. As the families are led to a secured area, Jennifer can't shake the feeling that their lives have just taken a dangerous turn. She steels herself, prepared to do whatever it takes to protect her family and find out the truth.

CHAPTER 9
THE PRICE OF LOYALTY

THE MAJESTIC SNOW-CAPPED peaks of the French Alps cast a stunning backdrop for a luxurious 18th-century villa nestled at their base. Teams of armed men patrol the lavish gardens, their eyes sharp and weapons at the ready.

Former US Presidents Daniel Taylor and William Morrison lounge by the pool, waiting for their elusive host. Taylor, more at ease in a ten-gallon hat sipping a Coors, checks his watch with a scowl, "Damn it, Bill. How much longer is he going to be? I have a flight to catch. It's not like when we were presidents with Air Force One waiting on standby."

Morrison, a Princeton graduate and Rhodes scholar known for his intolerance of fools, sips his cognac with deliberate slowness. "I'm sure it must pain you to fly commercial after being the leader of the free world."

Taylor glares at Morrison. "I'm sure he'll be along soon enough, Danny-boy. He knows we have a tight schedule."

"Fucking Europeans have no respect for other people's time!" Taylor grumbles.

"Patience, cowboy. Patience. Have you spoken to our military friend?"

Taylor nods. "Yes. He's a belligerent bastard, but everything is on schedule."

"Good. Our host will be pleased to hear that."

The head of Morrison's security team enters the pavilion. "Sir, Varennikov has just arrived."

"Thank you," Morrison replies.

Alexander Varennikov, head of the Russian Intelligence Agency (SVR), bursts onto the scene with a boisterous laugh. The large, imposing man tosses his coat at one of the attendants. "Ahhh, my good friends! I'm sorry to have kept you waiting. The UN Secretary-General pulled me aside at the conference just as I was leaving. He expressed his concern regarding our troop buildup along the Ukrainian and Chinese borders."

Varennikov signals to a young woman standing nearby. "Vodka!" The busty Swiss waitress rushes to the bar to fulfill his request. "I told him our military has conducted exercises in and around those areas for over 50 years and that he had nothing to worry about." He stretches his arm out as if receiving applause. ". . . And for some reason, he didn't believe me!"

The waitress returns with a glass of the villa's finest vodka. With a look of disgust, the Russian slaps it out of her hands, sending it flying into the pool. "Bring me the bottle, wench!" He slaps her on the ass as she retreats. The group erupts into raucous laughter.

Taylor, growing increasingly impatient, says, "Let's get started; we don't have all night."

"What's your hurry, gentlemen? The night is young!" Varennikov roars.

Morrison leans forward in his chair. "We have a concern."

The Russian slams a shot of vodka. "About?"

Taylor leans back in his chair. "The Chinese."

Varennikov chuckles as he takes a sip of his vodka. "The leases on the Caspian oil pipelines are signed and sealed. As long as you deliver the Devastators and the research team as promised, you're going to be astonishingly rich."

Morrison glances around, growing uneasy with the number of unfamiliar faces. "Let's discuss this in private."

Varennikov nods. "Of course, my friends. Follow me." He slams another shot and leads them to the library, a magnificent three-story archive filled with countless books and tomes, some dating back to the Roman Empire. Varennikov closes the doors behind them, and the American and Russian security teams take up positions around the royal grounds in an uneasy détente.

The presidential aircraft, Air Force One, enters its final approach, preparing to land at Andrews Air Force Base. The F-35 escorts peel away as the massive blue and white superjet touches down. The secret service moves the president's limousine, known as "The Beast", into position.

President Thomas Powell, a stocky, gray-haired man with piercing eyes, exits the flying fortress. His National Security Adviser, Brian Evans, waits for him at the bottom of the jetway. "Welcome home, Mr. President."

Not one for small talk, the president replies, "I hope you have good news for me, Brian."

"I'm afraid not, sir. The Chinese are still on full alert and are deploying their air carrier group to the South China Sea. They still believe that we're striking at their interests in and around Asia."

"Great. And you've had our ambassador explain that we're not involved, right?"

"Yes, Mr. President, but they ask if not us, then who?"

"That's a damn good question."

"And there's something else."

"What now?"

"The directors of the NSA and the CIA are waiting for you in your limo. They say it's urgent."

"It better be."

. . .

PRESIDENT POWELL SLIDES into the back of his limousine, where the directors of the two most powerful intelligence agencies on Earth sit quietly, ready to brief their commander-in-chief. NSA Director William Allen begins to speak, but the president silences him with a finger as he pours himself a scotch—neat.

The president, showing signs of a long overseas tour of the NATO alliance, looks like he hasn't slept in days. "Gentlemen, this had better be good. I have an international incident brewing, and I don't need any distractions."

"Sir, you need to see this." Allen hands President Powell a folder. Observing their body language, the president can tell it's serious. He thumbs through the folder.

"So, what am I looking at?"

CIA Director Eric Foster hands the president an additional series of photos. "Our assets covering the peace conference in Geneva took these photos of Daniel Taylor and William Morrison at a chalet near Lake Lausanne."

The president smirks. "And . . .? Is that it? Considering that these two hate each other, and there's plenty of reason for that, the fact that they're seen together doesn't rise to the level of a national security crisis. They could be on a skiing boondoggle for all we know."

"Take a look at the next few photos, sir."

He rifles through the next few images and finds a photo of the two ex-presidents with Varennikov in the pool area of the chalet. "Who's the third guy?"

"Alexander Varennikov, head of the Russian intelligence service. Our analysts are telling us that he's in line to be the next prime minister."

"Now you have my attention. What do we know?"

"Unfortunately, sir, not much. They were seen entering the chalet in the early evening. Taylor left first, followed by Morrison an hour later."

"What did they talk about?"

"We don't know. It was just by chance that we found them together at all."

"What about the Secret Service? Their protection detail must have something."

"No, sir. They both relinquished their protection last year. They have their own private security teams now," Foster adds.

The president gazes out the window as they pass the Lincoln Memorial. "The amount of damage these two have done to this country during their terms in office is immeasurable. War hawks to the end. Whatever they were talking about with the Russians can't be good."

"There are also some indications that they still have very strong ties to the more radical factions of our military," Foster states.

"Bill, I want you to increase surveillance on them. Individually, they're nothing to worry about, but together with their group of economic hitmen, they could create a perfect storm that could destroy everything that is still good about this country."

"Yes, sir."

"Now, tell me about the Chinese."

The president is briefed on the latest developments in the South China Sea. Satellite images reveal the Chinese air carrier group's movements and potential targets in the region.

"The Chinese are deploying an advanced air defense system around their carrier group," reports Allen. "It's designed to counter our stealth aircraft and cruise missiles."

"Any idea what they're after?" the president inquires.

"We believe they're protecting their interests in the South China Sea, particularly the disputed islands and the valuable resources beneath them. It's also a show of force to the neighboring countries and a deterrent against any potential US intervention."

The president rubs his temples, feeling the weight of the

world on his shoulders. "We need to find a way to de-escalate the situation and get the Chinese to stand down."

"It's not going to be easy, sir," Foster replies. "The Chinese are becoming increasingly assertive in the region. They won't back down without a diplomatic solution."

"I want a meeting with the Chinese ambassador as soon as possible," the president orders. "And get our negotiators working on a proposal that benefits both parties. We can't afford an armed conflict in Asia right now."

"Yes, Mr. President."

As the president's motorcade enters the gates of the White House, his thoughts turn to the photos of Taylor, Morrison, and Varennikov. He wonders what schemes they have planned and how they might affect the delicate balance of power on the world stage.

The geopolitical chess game continues, and President Powell knows he must stay several moves ahead to protect his country and maintain global stability. But with unpredictable players like Taylor, Morrison, and Varennikov in the mix, the stakes have never been higher, and one wrong move could lead to catastrophe.

CHAPTER 10
HIDDEN AGENDA

JENNIFER'S THOUGHTS drift as she gazes out of the second-story bedroom window. Young colts frolic and play in the sun-drenched fields beyond, their energy and innocence contrasting sharply with the armed men patrolling the perimeter of the farmhouse. A knock at the door pulls her back to reality.

"Come in," Jennifer calls, her voice wavering slightly.

A cart laden with burgers and pizza is wheeled into the room, momentarily capturing the attention of the children immersed in a video game. Chris, a dangerously handsome Russian mercenary with probing eyes and a facial scar that hints at his dangerous past in Chechnya, maneuvers the cart into the center of the room. Greg, his silent partner, stands by the door, his expression as cold and unyielding as granite.

Jennifer's unease grows, her voice firm but trembling, "I want to know who you are and why we're here."

"My name is Chris. This is Greg," Chris replies, his voice an unsettling mix of menace and charm. Greg remains stoic and unresponsive, his gaze never leaving Jennifer.

Matthew glances up from his game as he grabs a slice of pizza. "You don't look like a Chris."

Jennifer scrutinizes the two men, her maternal instincts on

high alert. Chris offers her a sly smile, but she remains undeterred.

"I demand an explanation. You abducted us from the banquet hall and brought us here without any explanation. And what about that explosion? Was it a terrorist attack?"

"Like I said before, Mrs. Simmons, you were brought here for your protection. A precaution to ensure your safety," Chris explains, his voice smooth as silk.

"Yeah, yeah, yeah. I want to know when we can leave. And I want to speak with my husband."

"I'm afraid that's not possible," Chris replies, his expression unyielding.

"I don't care! I want to speak to him . . . Now!" The tension in the room escalates, and the children look up from their game, sensing the brewing storm.

"Hey, why don't you guys finish eating in the other room?" Jennifer suggests, her voice strained. Apprehensively, the children roll the cart into the adjoining room and watch TV.

"Don't worry, Mrs. Simmons," Chris says, reaching out to her.

"Don't touch me!" Jennifer snaps, recoiling from his touch.

"There's no need to be afraid."

"I'm not afraid."

"We'll be taking you to see your husband tomorrow. There were . . . complications in his travel plans, so we're going to bring you to him."

"Oh, really?"

"Yes. Please be ready to leave by 0800 hours."

As Chris passes Greg in the doorway, he subtly taps him on the shoulder and directs his gaze across the room. Jennifer follows their gaze—what the fuck are you looking at? They're leering at her two young daughters, who are growing into beautiful young women. Chris whispers something to Greg, eliciting a vile snicker.

In an instant, Jennifer's protective instincts flare, and she moves to block their view, her expression a silent warning. Chris and Greg retreat, their laughter echoing down the hall. Jennifer quickly locks the door, relieved that they're gone for the time being.

She watches her children as they finish their meal, blissfully unaware of the danger lurking just outside their door. Her thoughts return to her husband, and she silently pleads for his safe return: Tony, where are you?

CHAPTER 11
THE WRAITH WITHIN

TONY AND SPENCER step out of the elevator on the 24th floor, their eyes scanning the sleek, polished hallway for office number 2418, where Adrianne's laboratory is located.

"There . . . on the right," Tony whispers, pointing to the door. Spencer retrieves a compact set of lock-picking tools from his pocket and, with the precision of a seasoned operative, quickly defeats the lock. Tony readies his .45-caliber pistol and cautiously pushes the door open.

"Stay behind me, and be quiet," he orders. Spencer nods silently, miming a zipping motion across his lips. As they enter the darkened office, they discover an expansive facility reminiscent of the clandestine research center they'd encountered in Uzbekistan.

"We need to find any information that can help you reconnect with your family. I'll start here. I saw a small office on the other side of the lab," Spencer suggests.

"I got it," Tony replies, his voice barely audible. Navigating through a labyrinth of cutting-edge equipment, Tony reaches the other side of the lab. He's taken aback by the striking collection of Greek mythological art adorning the walls. As he scans the paintings and statues, Tony's gaze lands on Goya's chilling depiction of Cronus devouring one of his children.

In the corner, he spots a statue of Perseus triumphantly holding Medusa's severed head. Tony sits behind Adrianne's immaculate desk and rifles through the drawers. He discovers a photograph of her family and several bottles of potent antipsychotic medications. As he reaches under the desk, he finds a hidden compartment. He presses a recessed button and finds a data imager.

Activating the device, a holographic video of a sun-soaked Caribbean beach materializes before him, complete with the sound of crashing waves. A couple emerges from the water, hand in hand, and races to a nearby towel. As they lie down and share a passionate kiss, the image pans to reveal Adrianne and . . . Tony himself.

"What the hell?" he mutters, dumbfounded. The holographic couple runs down the sandy beach, hand in hand, their laughter carrying on the wind.

Spencer appears in the doorway. "Did you find something?" he asks.

"This doesn't make sense. She has this holographic video of us together, but it never happened. Where did it come from?"

Spencer studies the scene. "It's too detailed for CGI. It looks like a memory fragment."

"But whose memory? This has to be fake. A forgery of some kind. What about you? Did you find anything?"

"No," Spencer admits, shaking his head.

"Damn it!" Tony exclaims, his frustration mounting.

"Don't worry, we'll get them back," Spencer reassures him.

Tony's anger boils over. "You don't know what you're talking about! You don't have kids! You don't know what it feels like to know they're in danger and there's nothing you can do about it! I was supposed to protect them! It was my job to protect them! And now they're gone!" As Tony's heart rate accelerates, he breaks out in a cold sweat, and the room begins to spin. His vision fades to black as a vision takes hold of his mind . . .

In a dense, humid jungle, a group of men convenes in a secluded tent flanked by heavily armed guards. A massive, amorphous entity materializes before them. The men rise slowly from their seats, their eyes wide with confusion and fear. Behind each man, vivid images from their lives flash like a personal highlight reel of their heinous deeds — murder, rape, torture. The collective weight of their evil deeds hangs heavy in the air. Suddenly, a piercing sound fills the tent, and each man screams in agony before exploding from within. The once pristine tent is now a grotesque tableau of flesh and bone.
A metallic voice whispers,
"We are one!"

Tony awakens with a start, disoriented.

"Another vision?" Spencer asks, concern etched on his face.

Tony nods, taking a moment to steady himself. "I'm sorry for what I said. It's not true."

"Part of it is," Spencer admits. "I may not know what it's like to have your family kidnapped, but I do know what it's like not to protect people who are depending on you. I don't have the resources to help you find them, but I know who does."

He helps Tony to his feet, their resolve strengthened.

"Let's get out of here. We have a date with the Devil."

CHAPTER 12
UNFORESEEN CONSEQUENCES

TONY AND SPENCER veer off the bustling main street and into a shadowy alley behind a row of seedy bars. They slowly come to a stop in front of a nondescript club, "Stolovaya." The exterior exudes an air of danger, with armed guards and an array of surveillance cameras scanning the vicinity.

"So, how many times have you been here?" Tony asks, his gaze scanning the building's exterior.

"Been here?" Spencer stammers. "Why would I have been here? This is a dangerous place. Not for someone like me. I could get . . . spit on . . . or something worse."

"You told me these guys could help us hack into the S.Y.N.C. central core. How many times have you dealt with them?"

"Well . . . none, per se. I know a guy who did some work for a friend of his whose brother works here. He said their setup makes the NSA's systems look like a PlayStation."

Tony rubs his face with both hands, incredulous. "So, you expected us to just walk into what's probably the North American headquarters for the Russian mafia and ask to use their computers? Like an internet café?"

"Ummm . . . well . . . yeah . . . sort of."

Tony scrutinizes the club's entrance, taking note of the four armed guards and the array of surveillance cameras. "And why would they let us do that?"

"Because you have something they want."

"Which is?"

"Your brain!"

"I knew this was a bad idea." Tony shifts the car into gear.

"Wait! Hear me out. You have the most sophisticated cybernetic interface on the planet. It's state-of-the-art US military technology, and it's worth billions!"

"Spencer, I told you already. It's fried. I can't connect to anything with it now. The lights are on, but no one's home."

"Yeah, but they don't know that! Once we get into the S.Y.N.C. core, we can . . ." Spencer hesitates.

"We can what?"

"Ummm . . . I don't know yet. We can figure it out when we get what we need."

"That's it? That's your plan? Figure it out when we're surrounded by an angry mob of Russian gangsters armed with Kalashnikovs?"

"Mostly."

"OK. We're leaving."

Just as Tony begins to drive away, three of the guards step in front of the car and aim their rifles at the windshield. The largest among them approaches the driver's side window and taps the glass with the barrel of his rifle. Tony reluctantly rolls down the window.

"Who are you?" the guard demands in a heavy Russian accent.

"Nobody. We're just leaving."

"No. I think you were just staying. Who are you? And why have you been sitting here for so long?"

"Listen, comrade, we don't want any trouble. So, if you don't mind, we'll be on our way."

"You don't want trouble?" the guard smirks. "But trouble wants you!"

The other guards laugh while Tony's grip on the steering wheel tightens.

"Tony, don't!"

He takes a deep breath. "We're here to see . . ."

"Dimitri," Spencer interjects.

". . . Dimitri. I have something he'll be very interested in seeing."

"Alex the Fox sent us," Spencer adds.

"Who?" The guard's brow furrows.

Tony shakes his head.

"Alex . . . ! The Fox!," Spencer repeats.

The guards charge their weapons and take aim.

"Oh, God . . ." Spencer crosses himself.

A radio crackles.

"What the fuck is going on? Who's out there?" Dimitri's voice demands in Russian. The guard reaches for the radio on his shoulder and keys the mic.

"These two guys want to see you. They said Alex sent them."

A tense silence stretches out.

"Kill them," Dimitri orders.

The guards raise their weapons . . .

"Wait!"

Another pause.

"Send them down. I want to see for myself."

Reluctantly, the guards yank Tony and Spencer out of the car.

"I told you we would get in!" Spencer exclaims.

"Getting in isn't what I'm worried about," Tony mutters as the guards shove them down a narrow, dimly lit passageway. They pass more armed guards and finally enter a sprawling, dark cyber data center. "It's getting out again."

TONY AND SPENCER stand before Dimitri Romanov, the infamous Russian crime lord, in his clandestine den of cyber thieves. These elite hackers are on the U.S. Cyber Command's most wanted list, and their lair is an electrifying mix of shadows and the hum of powerful computers.

"So, who sent you?" Dimitri's voice is like gravel, his eyes like ice.

"Alex," Tony lies smoothly, keeping his face impassive.

"The Fox!" Spencer adds, eager to provide the necessary clarification.

Dimitri snorts. "Alex owes me money. I hate it when someone owes me something and doesn't deliver. They usually pay with their life. Why are you here?"

"I want you to hack into S.Y.N.C. Headquarters," Tony demands, his voice steady.

The room full of hackers pauses, exchanging glances, then erupts into raucous laughter. The air is thick with derision and disbelief.

"I need you to search their databases for a highly classified project," Tony continues.

"Really? And do you want fries and a shake with that?" Dimitri smirks, relishing the chance to use the American idiom. The laughter intensifies.

"I'm serious," Tony insists.

Dimitri moves to stand inches from Tony's face, his breath hot and foul. "So am I! Are you insane? You must know what you're asking is impossible. Their firewalls and intrusion detection systems are beyond state-of-the-art. Virtually impenetrable. We also have a cozy agreement with the American intelligence services, especially S.Y.N.C. We don't hack into their classified systems, and they don't lase us into dust with one of their space-based weapons!"

"So you can't do it?" Tony challenges.

"I didn't say 'can't.' What's in it for me? I know you didn't come down here empty-handed."

"I have stolen S.Y.N.C. hardware. I'm willing to give you access to it."

"Show me."

Tony brushes up his hair and reveals an array of blue strobing lights. The hackers fall silent, their awe palpable. Ivan, Dimitri's right-hand man, steps forward and speaks in hushed tones with his boss.

"A subcranial cybernetic interface. Impressive. What is your offer?"

"I'll let you jack in and map the computing circuitry if you get me into S.Y.N.C."

"What are you looking for?"

"I'll know when I find it. Do we have a deal?"

Dimitri consults with Ivan. "We'll have to destroy our data center afterward. Once their intrusion detection picks us up, we'll have 30 minutes to get out of here before their assault teams arrive."

"That sounds like your problem, not mine." Tony's voice is steely.

Dimitri glares at him, weighing his options. "Alright, you have a deal. Getting just a glimpse at the circuitry on that chip can put me years ahead of my competition. Then net-raiding will be like taking candy from a baby."

The group of hackers hones their focus on the task at hand, skillfully defeating the complicated series of security zones. They quickly locate the diagrams and schematics for the advanced weapons division.

"Impressive. You and your friends have been busy," Dimitri comments, his voice laced with grudging admiration.

"Show me who's working in the command center."

"That's a different system. We don't have access yet," Ivan replies.

As the hackers continue their work, Spencer notices a local news report. "Hey, turn that up," he says.

Ivan increases the volume, and the newscaster's voice fills the room: "This is News Channel 7 coming to you with an exclusive report. A banquet hall outside of Alexandria is burning out of control. Our Lisa Myers is on the scene."

"I'm here with Barbara Collins from the Defense Department's Family Affairs office. Can you tell us what happened?" Myers asks.

"It was horrible! We were having a welcome home party for our service members returning from overseas, and there was the smell of gas. Before we knew it, everyone was overcome by the fumes. I barely made it outside, then there was this massive explosion." Barbara cries uncontrollably as firefighters remove bodies from the devastation.

Myers continues, "As you can see, this tragedy has affected many in the military community. We have unconfirmed reports that there were as many as 32 servicemen and their families trapped inside."

"Tony, this was about the time your convoy was hit. Do you think it was your team?" Spencer asks, concern etching his face.

"I don't know," Tony replies, his voice tense.

"You know, I'm sorry about your friends, but we're running out of time. Ivan, hook up to his interface so we can get the hell out of here. Listen up, everyone! Burn it down!" Dimitri orders.

The group scrambles and begins the evacuation process. They start to destroy the equipment with axes and erase the data arrays. Strips of ferrite located strategically around the room are lit. They slice through the equipment racks like butter, reducing everything inside to liquid metal and showering the room with white-hot sparks.

"Wait!" Tony interrupts. He takes a picture out of his wallet and hands it to Dimitri. "I want you to do a facial scan of the area for my family." Dimitri hesitates.

"If you don't, the deal is off."

He gives the photo to Ivan. "Do it fast!"

Ivan scans the photo and uses a facial recognition program to search the entire closed-circuit video system. "I got a hit. They entered the hall, but everyone was put on buses just before the blast."

"Then they're still alive! Where were they being taken?" Tony demands.

Dimitri has had enough. "Stop, you're done now! We're out of time. Give me access to the interface!"

Spencer blurts out, "Oh boy . . ."

Dimitri grabs Tony and throws him to the ground as Ivan places an induction connector behind Tony's head and starts the mapping program. After a few moments . . .

"Boss, there's nothing there."

"What?" Dimitri snarls.

"The power is on, but the circuit is fried."

"You bastard! You lied to me! I'm going to blow your fucking head off!"

Dimitri pulls out a gold-plated .50 Cal Desert Eagle from his underarm holster. It gleams brightly as the ferrite sparks continue to shower the room. Tony stares down the enormous barrel with nowhere to run. "Unlike you, you piece of shit, a gun means what it says!"

The facial scan completes, and a wanted poster with Tony's picture pops up on Ivan's display. "Boss! Wait! I just got a hit on this guy. He's wanted by the Department of Homeland Security. A two-million-dollar reward."

Dimitri's smile returns. "So this might not be a total loss after all. Tie him and his friend up. Let's get the hell out of here. The explosives are set to blow in 10 minutes."

Ivan moves to handcuff Tony, but Tony head-butts him and slips him into a stranglehold, then snaps his neck. Dimitri fires his hand cannon.

"Watch out!" Spencer shouts. Spencer tackles Dimitri as the gun goes off. The massive slug whistles past Tony's head as he ducks. He rolls across the floor and jumps up to meet the approaching guards. He cuts his way through them like a buzzsaw. Blood and the sickening sound of broken bones trail behind him.

A hacker, hiding behind a desk, summons his courage and hits Tony with a TASER, dropping him to his knees. Dimitri pushes Spencer off of him and walks over to Tony as he writhes in pain from the 50,000 volts coursing through his body.

"This is for Ivan." Dimitri lands a right hook, knocking Tony out cold. "Take them out of here. This place is going to blow."

The remaining criminals make it to the vehicles parked behind the club. They throw Tony and Spencer in the back of one of the vans. The whistling sound of rappelling rope fills the air as men drop like silent predators onto the ground around the Russians. They kill them all with ninja-like precision. They grab Tony and Spencer from the van and take them to an awaiting truck.

"I'm so glad you guys got here in time. They were going to kill us, or worse! I can explain why we hacked your network, I swear!" Spencer pleads.

The leader grabs Spencer by the throat and injects him with a powerful tranquilizer. He shouts in Chinese to the driver.

"Who are youuuu . . .?" Spencer's voice fades as he loses consciousness. As they drive away, the Russian data center erupts in a series of explosions, reducing the entire structure to rubble.

A NOTE FROM TONY

"Stories have to be told or they die, and when they die, we can't remember who we are or why we're here." – Sue Monk Kidd

Dear Reader,

I hope you never have to know what it feels like to have your family's lives hanging in the balance.

Being able to command the Devastators has always been both a blessing and a curse… To be able to control anything with your mind – there's always going to be someone else who wants that power… Of course, now it's my only hope of getting my family back, and I'll stop at nothing.

I know my mission, and I'm on it… But I'd like to ask you a favor too. No story is complete until it's been heard, and I want as many people to hear mine as possible. You can help me with that.

You may not be able to help me connect to the Devastators, but you *can* help me connect to other readers.

You in?

By leaving a review of this book on Amazon, you'll take my story to new eyes and ears – you'll make my struggles worth it.

Simply by letting other readers know how much you're enjoying the ride, you'll help get my story out to more people – and lead them to a gripping read in the process.

Thank you for your support. Now… Let's get back to it… We have work to do!

- Tony

CHAPTER 13
ALL OR NOTHING

CHRIS STANDS IMPATIENTLY at the bottom of the jetway, eyes scanning the scene before him. The kidnapped members of the research team are being rushed across the tarmac like frightened cattle, their hearts pounding in their chests as they try to keep pace with their captors. Chris counts them, trying to maintain order in his mind as he pushes them forward.

"We're running late! Keep them moving!" he barks, urgency evident in his voice.

The gunmen herd the hostages along, trying to keep their movements discreet and draw as little attention as possible. Jennifer Simmons holds her children close, her eyes darting around, searching for a chance to escape. The wind picks up, and in that moment, the jacket of one of the gunmen flutters open, revealing a holstered Beretta M9.

Years of training kick in for Jennifer. She strikes the gunman in the lower leg with a swift kick, causing him to drop to one knee. Seizing the opportunity, she snatches the weapon and aims it at Chris.

"Stop! Stop right now!" she demands, her voice shaking but firm.

The remaining gunmen whirl around, their own concealed

weapons now trained on her. Chris slowly raises his hands, a malicious smirk forming on his lips.

"You know you can be arrested for bringing a loaded weapon into an airport?" he taunts, extending a hand toward her. "There's no sense in fighting now. Your fates are sealed. Give me the gun."

"No! This is as far as we're going," Jennifer says, her resolve strengthening. "Tell your men to put their guns down. Now!"

The bustling airport seems to continue around them, oblivious to the tense standoff taking place. Jets taxi in the distance, the noise of their engines filling the air.

"Look around you, Mrs. Simmons," Chris sneers. "There's no place to go. Put down the gun, and no one will get hurt."

Jennifer's attention is momentarily drawn to one of the gunmen as he begins to move toward her. She fires a shot in Chris's direction, barely missing his ear. The families around her drop to the ground, panic sets in.

"We're not going any farther. Put your guns down and walk away!" Jennifer yells, her voice cracking with emotion.

"You stupid bitch! I don't have time for this!" Chris spits, his anger boiling over.

As the confrontation unfolds, Greg creeps up behind Jennifer and grabs her son Matthew. The boy struggles, kicking and screaming as he is pulled closer to the deafening roar of the jet's idling engine.

"Matthew!" Jennifer cries, her aim shifting from Chris to Greg.

"What you fail to understand," Chris says, his voice cold and malicious, "is that you are all just commodities to me." He takes a step closer to Jennifer, eyes never leaving her face. "One more or less doesn't make a difference to me. You're all like stray dogs. In my country, we shoot stray dogs or, in this case . . ." Greg hoists Matthew off the ground, the boy's legs flailing wildly in the air. ". . . Throw them into jet engines!"

Jennifer's eyes widen in horror as she sees the terror on her son's face, his sisters watching on, petrified. Her arms trembling, she begins to lower the gun.

Seizing the opportunity, Chris lunges forward and snatches the gun from Jennifer's hand, sending her sprawling onto the tarmac with a vicious backhand.

"Just as I thought. You're weak, like all Americans," he sneers. "You might have succeeded if you were willing to sacrifice one for the good of the many."

He grabs Jennifer by the hair, yanking her to her feet. "Try something like that again, and I will torture you in front of your children in ways you can't imagine. What lovely scars that would leave them with."

With a forceful shove, he throws her back in line with the others. The children rush to their mother's arms, tears streaming down their faces.

"You idiots! Get them moving!" Chris barks at his men. "We're running behind schedule because of your stupidity! If we miss the train, I will shoot you all myself!"

Under Chris's watchful eye, Jennifer and her children are roughly pushed onto one of the charter buses, along with the rest of the kidnapped researchers. The vehicle speeds out of the airport, its tires squealing as it heads toward the Moscow railway station.

A tense silence fills the bus, the weight of their situation settling heavily on the shoulders of the hostages. Jennifer holds her children close, her mind racing with possible plans for escape. Through the window, she glimpses the Kremlin's fortified walls and the imposing domes of St. Basil's Cathedral. She knows that in order to save her family and the others, she would have to muster all the strength and courage she possesses. Time was running out, and their lives hung in the balance.

CHAPTER 14
THE IMPOSSIBLE TRUTH

THE ROAR of engines fills the air as three black vans tear down the interstate before veering off onto a secluded dirt road. Dust billows behind the speeding vehicles, forming a thick cloud that threatens to swallow them whole. The vans continue their mad dash down the narrow road until they reach their destination: a desolate farmhouse in rural Maryland.

As the first rays of dawn break over the horizon, the farm seems to shudder beneath the weight of the events that will soon unfold within its walls.

Inside the farmhouse, Tony and Spencer find themselves bound to wooden chairs, their wrists chafing against the rough rope that hold them captive. Hoods cover their heads, blocking out any light and leaving them in complete darkness. They can hear the faint sounds of footsteps, the murmurs of conversation, and the occasional scrape of metal against metal—as if someone was sharpening a knife.

The door creaks open, and a man steps into the room, his boots thudding against the worn wooden floorboards as he approaches the captives. The man, Jike, gestures to one of his soldiers, who yanks the hoods from Tony and Spencer's heads.

The floodlights overhead blaze to life, blinding the two men as they squint into the onslaught of light. The harsh illumination exposes the room's shabby state: peeling wallpaper, cracked plaster, and the detritus of abandonment.

"Welcome, gentlemen," Jike says, his voice smooth and confident. He moves to stand directly in front of Tony, staring down at him with a mixture of curiosity and disdain. "It's an honor to finally meet you face to face, major."

Tony meets Jike's gaze, refusing to shield his eyes from the blinding light. "Who are you?" he demands, his voice a low growl.

"I am your pursuer, your nemesis. You have proven to be quite an elusive prey," Jike replies with a sinister smile. His eyes gleam like a predator closing in on its quarry.

"So you're the one tracking me?" Tony asks, his voice barely masking his anger.

"Yes. Yes, I am," Jike confirms.

"The attack on the convoy? At my home? The ambulance?"

"Yes, major. But even before that. My country is well aware of your drone program and has been for quite some time," Jike reveals, the shadows in the room accentuating the cold determination on his face.

"That's impossible!" Tony spits. "Without their digital signatures, the Devastators are invisible to all detection systems. They're light-years ahead of anything in your arsenal, and you know it."

Jike nods in agreement. "Yes, major. Tracking the drones themselves is quite impossible."

"Then how?" Tony growls, his frustration mounting.

"You have a traitor in your midst," Jike says, his voice dripping with menace. "By breaking his encrypted communications, we've been able to track the drones' activities, if not the drones themselves."

Jike turns his head to show Tony the neural connections in the back of his neck. "My mission is to imprint your neural net, take control of the drones, and then kill the remaining members of the research team."

Tony's eyes widen, and he strains against his bonds, trying in vain to free himself. His captors hold him down, smirking as they watch him struggle. "You kidnapped my family! If you hurt any of them, I swear . . ."

"I didn't take your family, major," Jike interrupts, his voice cold and impassive.

"You're a fucking liar!" Tony shouts, his face reddening with fury.

"I am many things, major. A patriot, a loyal servant to the citizens of my country. A liar is not one of them," Jike says. "If I had taken them, you would know."

"Then who? Why?" Tony demands, his eyes narrowing as he searches Jike's face for any hint of deception.

"Finding the why will most assuredly lead you to who," Jike replies cryptically.

Tony twists his massive shoulder, freeing himself from his captors, his hands still tied. Jike continues questioning him, a hint of curiosity in his tone. "What did those Russian gangsters want with you?"

"The same as you, access to my neural net. But they found out the hard way, it was fried by an E.M.P. spike. I have no way to connect to the Devastators, and neither will you," Tony replies confidently.

Xiao, Jike's trusted lieutenant, pulls out a sensor and waves it over Tony's head. "It's true, colonel. All of his cybernetic circuits have been completely destroyed."

Tony grins. "I guess that kinda fucks things up for you, doesn't it?"

Jike remains unphased. "But the digital signatures are still intact, correct?"

Xiao nods. "Yes, colonel."

Jike circles Tony slowly, then bends down to be directly in his face. "No, major. I suspected that was the case once we detected the E.M.P. strike. With the possibility of you falling into the hands of their enemies, how could your government let you be compromised? It was a possibility I had already considered."

He pauses for a moment. "With no one able to control the drones, I can now focus on the second half of my mission."

Spencer can't help but inquire. "Which is?"

Jike grabs Tony's shirt, pulling him closer. "Do you know why you're still alive?"

Tony smirks. "My cheery disposition?"

Jike smiles back. "No, major. For me to complete my mission, the S.Y.N.C. command center must be destroyed, and you're going to help me do just that."

Tony scoffs, "Really? You know, I thought your government banned the opium trade. Because you must be high if you think I'm going to help you."

Jike remains calm. "On the contrary, major, I am quite lucid. You're the one who's not thinking clearly."

"Enlighten me," Tony challenges.

Jike's eyes narrow. "Think about it. Who exactly disconnected you from the drones and destroyed your neural interface?"

Tony remains silent, his brow furrowing as he contemplates Jike's words.

Jike continues, pressing the point, "If I didn't kidnap your family and comrades, then who? And more importantly, why? You have far more enemies than in this room, major. The truth is that the drones, and your team, are soon to be in the hands of madmen. Now our missions are one and the same: to destroy the Devastator program."

Spencer chimes in, his voice cautious, "He may have a point, Tony."

Jike nods. "Listen to your friend."

Tony remains defiant. "Even if I was to believe half the shit you're peddling, how can I trust you?"

Jike replies with a well-known adage, "It has been said, 'The enemy of my enemy is my friend.'"

Tony's expression remains unyielding. "Thanks for the advice, Sun Tsu, or whatever the fuck your name is. Now get this through your thick skull: I'm never going to help you! And if I could right now, I would hand you a good old-fashioned American ass-whipping and send your sorry ass to see whatever deity or duck you expect to meet in the hereafter."

One of Jike's lieutenants moves forward to punish Tony for his insult, but Jike gestures for him to stand down. "So you are a man of honor. Willing to back up your words with deeds. Commendable. It's a shame our leaders do not understand this concept."

Jike moves slowly to his left, then orders, "Untie his hands."

Xiao hesitates.

"Do it!" Jike commands.

Tony steps away from Spencer as he and Jike begin to circle each other like a lion sizing up a tiger. They freeze, each holding a perfect fighting stance.

Tony releases a primal yell and rushes forward, unleashing a hurricane of deadly strikes. Jike expertly blocks every strike, as if swatting flies out of the air. Tony spins low in a foot sweep, but Jike jumps and delivers a flying side kick to Tony's head, driving him back several feet.

"Your power is your weakness, major. You fight with rage. In the end, your emotions will defeat you," Jike taunts.

Tony clenches his fists tighter, more determined than ever. He lunges at Jike with more precision, forcing him to defend more quickly until he finally catches Jike with a wheel kick that knocks him back onto his hands and knees. Jike's men move to help him, but he gestures them away.

"You should've packed a lunch. This may take a while," Tony taunts as Jike spits blood onto the floor and rises to his feet.

"Your days have come to an end, major," Jike responds coldly.

Jike sprints toward Tony, and as he throws a right hook, he slides under it, coming up behind Tony and delivering an elbow to the back of his head that sends him stumbling forward. Blow after blow finds its mark as Tony is unable to defend against Jike's vicious cybernetically enhanced onslaught. Finally, a roundhouse kick sends him down for good.

"Tony! Get up! He's coming!" Spencer shouts, but it's too late.

Crawling away, Jike grabs Tony by the hair and turns him over, then lifts him by the collar. He begins to hit Tony with full-force punches, one bone-shattering blow after another. The sickening thuds echo through the room.

"Stop! Stop it! You're killing him!" Spencer screams, but Jike continues relentlessly.

Finally, Xiao steps forward. "Sifu . . ."

Jike stops mid-strike, and Xiao continues, "We still need him . . . alive."

Jike looks down at Tony, bloody and semi-unconscious, and realizes Xiao is right. He tosses Tony to the ground, and Spencer frees himself and rushes to his friend's side.

"Take them away," Jike orders, and his men drag Tony and Spencer to the back of the farmhouse, locking them in a root cellar. Spencer cradles Tony's head as his mind drifts. . .

An airliner cruising high above the sea is accompanied by fighter jets. Suddenly large hands, as if from God himself, reach across the sky and grab the fighters as if they were toys, then crush them effortlessly. The airliner dives in an attempt to escape. It's grabbed violently by the fuselage. The strain of the engines, as they race to full throttle, is deafening. The terrified faces of the passengers can be seen through the windows. The God-like hands then snap the jet in two, causing a huge explosion. The wreckage and bodies fall slowly, ghost-like, to the sea below. Adrianne's voice, "WE ARE ONE!"

As the sun sets, Tony regains consciousness, wincing as he touches his bruised and battered face. Spencer had done his best to tend to his wounds with the bandages their captors had provided.

"You were talking in your sleep. Another vision?" Spencer asks.

Tony groans "Yeah. Some sort of attack on an airliner. These huge hands just crushed it. It felt like mine, but . . ."

"I think I've figured out what's causing them," Spencer says, but Tony cuts him off.

"I'll tell you what's causing them: I'm fucking losing my mind!"

"No. Listen, they started after the E.M.P. strike fried the interface, right?" Spencer argues. "I think the shock to your brain has released some masked memories."

"Are you saying that someone purposely blocked parts of my memory from me?" Tony asks, incredulous.

"Yes," Spencer insists. "I don't think that they're dreams or visions. I think that they're real events that were purposely locked away in your memory somehow."

As they sit in the dimly lit root cellar, Spencer explains, "Before you showed up on my porch full of bullet holes, I was hacking into the NSA intel reports, and there have been several incidents that are very similar to your visions."

"Similar in what way?" Tony asks.

"Well, one was involving an interdiction strike in the desert of Mongolia, where a high-ranking Chinese general was killed before delivering vital supplies to a Chinese installation under attack. Because the supplies never made it, the installation fell to Russian mercenaries."

"That was my first vision!" Tony exclaims.

"It gets better," Spencer continues. "A group of ruthless rebels in Central America, loyal to the Chinese government, were mysteriously killed in the jungle just before mounting an attack to overthrow their government. This would have given China a firm foothold in the Americas."

"Now it's all starting to make sense," Tony says. "Someone

has been using the Devastators through me to conduct these clandestine missions to start a covert war."

"Well, it's not going to be covert for long," Spencer warns. "Your last vision says it all. A few days ago, an airliner went down carrying the president of Taiwan. He was heading to a summit in Beijing to sign a defense agreement which would have eliminated all U.S. military forces from Taiwan."

"You're right, it's already begun," Tony agrees.

"But who? Everyone that was part of the program is either dead or kidnapped."

"I don't know, but the answer is at S.Y.N.C. Headquarters. We have to get in," Tony declares.

"Yeah, good luck with that," Spencer replies, skeptical of their chances.

"There is one way," Tony says, walking to the door and banging loudly. A guard silently appears. "I want to speak to Jike."

The guard eyes them both, then radios the request. Spencer couldn't hide his concern. "Tony, you can't be serious. He just tried to kill you."

"You heard what he said, 'The enemy of my enemy . . .'" Tony begins.

". . . is my friend," Spencer finishes reluctantly, realizing that Tony was right. To get the answers they need, they have no choice but to form an uneasy alliance with their captor.

CHAPTER 15
FALLOUT

BLACK TACTICAL VANS slice through the night, their powerful LED headlights tearing a path down the winding country road. The sinister amber glow of S.Y.N.C. Headquarters looms ahead like a malevolent specter. The convoy comes to a sudden halt, three vans assembling in a moonlit clearing several hundred meters from the fortified gate. Jike disembarks from the lead vehicle with his team. Tony and Spencer remain behind in the third van, its engine idling quietly.

"Spencer, when I give you the signal, do it just like we planned," Tony instructs, his voice firm and steady.

Spencer smiles nervously, a bead of sweat rolls down his temple. "I will."

Tony claps him on the back, his expression reassuring. "Don't worry, you got this."

As they exit the van, the teams gather around Tony and Jike. Jike's gaze is intense as he speaks.

"You have 15 minutes to disable their defense systems and open the front barriers."

"I know what I have to do," Tony responds, his voice conveying determination.

Spencer adjusts Tony's stealth suit, his hands trembling

slightly. "Remember, constant steady movement. No jerking around. If you move too quickly, the processors in the adaptive camouflage won't be able to keep up, and you'll be seen."

"It's okay, Spencer. I'll be fine," Tony reassures him. But Spencer continues to check the suit nervously.

"This isn't like last time. The suit's been upgraded. Trust me," Tony promises.

"Please be careful. I don't want to lose you like the others," Spencer pleads, his eyes filled with worry.

"You're the best at what you do, Spencer. Remember that." With that, Tony activates the stealth suit and moves toward the massive complex. As the suit shimmers, he disappears from sight.

TONY SLIPS past the front gate of S.Y.N.C. Headquarters, a phantom in the darkness. He subdues several guards and security personnel on his way to the power station. Setting the final charges, he triggers the explosives that cut the main line to the facility. In a cascading sequence, the facility plunges into darkness, taking the computer-controlled snipers offline and allowing access to the front gate.

"Moving to checkpoint Zulu. E.T.A. 5 minutes," Tony reports, his voice barely a whisper.

"Acknowledged," Jike's voice crackles in his earpiece.

Inside S.Y.N.C. Headquarters, Tony races at full speed, his breaths coming in short gasps as he navigates the maze-like complex. Rounding the last corner, he finds himself before a three-foot-thick beryllium alloy door. He mutters, "Abandon hope all ye who enter here..." as he works with a digital sequencer to crack the sophisticated encryption locking the massive gateway. A series of loud metallic clicks echo through the corridor as the door swings open, revealing the ominous darkness beyond.

Perched on the upper observation level of the command center, Tony surveys the scene below: a group huddles around a control panel, flanked by a heavily armed security detail. He creeps forward, his stealth suit rendering him invisible, and slips past the security team unnoticed. At the heart of the group, Tony deactivates his suit and draws his sidearm.

"Don't move!" he shouts, startling the group. A woman turns, her face a mix of shock and relief.

"Tony!" she gasps, her voice barely a whisper.

Time stands still.

"Adrianne? I thought you were..." Tony trails off, unable to finish the thought.

"...dead?" a man sneers, interrupting.

"Adelay!" Tony's eyes widen in disbelief. "I saw you, both of you... dead!"

Adelay smirks, the corners of his mouth twisting with malice. "You can't always trust your eyes, Tony. They're easily deceived."

"So, it's been you all along!" Tony accuses, his voice strained with anger.

"Of course, who else?" Adelay taunts. "I'm surprised it took you this long to figure it out." Tony turns to Adrianne, hurt and confusion written across his face. "Adrianne? How could you?"

"No, Tony! I tried to stop him, but..." Adrianne's voice trembles, her eyes pleading for understanding.

"Shut up! This is all your fault! You betrayed me!" Adelay roars, his face contorting with rage.

"I told you by destroying Tony's cybernetics there was no telling how the Devastators would respond," Adrianne counters.

Tony's jaw clenches in frustration. "What's happening?"

"We can't connect to them," Adrianne admits.

Adelay pulls a Glock 19 and presses it against Adrianne's temple, his finger twitching on the trigger. "Listen to me! You better find a way and do it fast!"

With his gun still trained on Adelay, Tony spits, "You bastard! You set this up from the beginning! You betrayed us all!"

"Your myopic view of the world is pathetic. You have no idea who or what you're dealing with!" Adelay snarls back, his eyes cold and calculating.

"I'm dealing with murderers and traitors!" Tony roars, his anger reaching a boiling point. With lightning speed, an enraged Tony catches Adelay with an elbow, sending his Glock skittering across the floor. A second blow puts him down on one knee.

"WHERE'S MY FAMILY? If anything has happened to them..."

Adelay wipes blood from a cut over his eye, his voice dripping with contempt. "Your family is fine."

"WHERE ARE THEY! If you've hurt them in any way, I'll gut you like a fucking pig!" Tony threatens, his eyes burning with fury.

"Relax. I'm not a monster," Adelay responds coolly, as if enjoying Tony's torment.

A vicious right cross finds Adelay's jaw. "WHERE!"

Adelay spits blood, his voice strained but defiant. "In Russia. The SVR has repatriated the entire team and their families to Moscow."

"Why?" Tony demands, his voice shaking with a mixture of rage and concern.

"They're going to create their own advanced cybernetics weapons program with neural nets and all," Adelay reveals, smirking as he divulges his plan.

"What kind of madmen kidnap women and children?" Tony seethes, his fists clenched at his sides.

"Kidnapped scientists work better when their families are with them. Plus, it gives them leverage. Your family will be waiting for you when you cooperate," Adelay explains, his voice chillingly matter-of-fact.

Adelay rises from his knee and delivers a crushing uppercut that knocks Tony back on his heels. The two face off, their eyes locked in a deadly stare.

"Stop!" Adrianne screams, stepping between them.

The command center shudders violently as an explosion tears through the room, sending debris and shrapnel flying in every direction. The sound of heavy boots fills the air as Jike's men rush in, surrounding everyone. Jike himself steps through the smoke and debris, his presence as imposing as a phantom.

"Who the hell is this?" Adelay demands, his eyes narrowing with suspicion.

"Ahhh... the venerable General Smith. The rumors of your demise seem to have been exaggerated," Jike says, his voice dripping with sarcasm. He walks enticingly close to Adrianne, adding, "As well as those of the lovely Doctor."

Tony's mind races, his voice urgent. "Jike, we're running out of time. We have to find..."

But as he moves towards the command console, Jike's men train their rifles on him.

"Not so fast, Major," Jike warns.

"You bastard! We had a deal!" Tony shouts, his anger boiling over.

Jike appears nonchalant. "Which I fulfilled by helping you enter S.Y.N.C. and securing the command center."

As Jike's men begin to place explosive charges around the room, Adelay realizes the truth. "So, you attacked the convoy."

"Yes," Jike confirms. "A sloppy operation you seemed to have been lucky enough to escape. You will not be so lucky this time."

Adelay scoffs. "Tony, you shouldn't have trusted these maniacs, they have no honor."

"That's a riot coming from you," Tony shot back.

Tears fill Adrianne's eyes as she apologizes. "Tony, I'm sorry. I'm so sorry. I should've told you the moment I found out what they were up to. They threatened to kill you. I couldn't bear that. Please forgive me."

"Enough! All of you! Turn around! Down on your knees!" Jike barks. Resigned to their fate, the group complies.

Adelay glares at Jike. "You're never going to make it out of this country alive. Delta Force will hunt you down like the dogs you are."

Jike bends close to Adelay's ear, his voice a chilling whisper. "This was always a one-way trip for my team. But today, I will take great satisfaction knowing that I was the one who sent you to Hell!"

Tony whispers into his hidden microphone. "Spencer, can you hear me?"

From the tactical van, with two unconscious Chinese commandos at his feet, Spencer responds, "Yes!"

"When I give you the signal, power up the sentinels," Tony instructs.

"Roger that!" Spencer replies, poised for action.

Jike saunters over to Tony, his voice menacing. "So, Major, all I need now are the digital signatures of the Devastators."

"Looks like you've been smoking that shit again. That's not going to happen!" Tony snarls.

In response, Jike drags Adrianne up by her hair, a knife presses against her throat. "Don't make me ask you again, Major. The gurgling of life leaving her body will be most unpleasant."

"Tony, don't!" Adrianne cries out, struggling under Jike's powerful grip.

Tony's fists clench, his voice filled with defiance. "Why don't you pick on somebody your own size?"

Jike throws Adrianne to the ground and marches toward Tony, intent on finishing what he had started.

"Spencer, now!" Tony shouts.

At his command, Spencer activates the sniper bots. Hidden panels around the room fly open, revealing mobile robots equipped with dual mini rail guns that roll onto the command center floor. Using facial recognition, they swiftly determine friend or foe, taking out five of Jike's men in a single salvo.

Tony grabs Adrianne and sprints towards the exit as everyone in the room scrambles for cover. Adelay's security team encircles him, fighting their way out. One by one, the sniper-bots systematically eliminated targets.

From behind a barricade, Jike takes out two of the sniper-bots before spotting Tony and Adrianne making their escape. Like a ninja, he climbs the surrounding structure and intercepts them.

"We have unfinished business, Major," Jike snarls.

Tony moves Adrianne behind him, his voice resolute. "Let's do this!"

Jike lunges forward, delivering several powerful overhead strikes. Tony manages to block each one but quickly realizes he is outmatched. With every blow, he and Adrianne are forced farther back until they reach the end of the platform.

"Would you like to tell her goodbye before I kill you?" Jike taunts.

"No need, because we're walking out of here," Tony retorts.

"I think that you've finally lost your mind, Major," Jike sneers.

"Think again," Tony counters, gesturing behind him.

Two of the sniper-bots take up position behind Jike. Unfazed, Jike remarks, "So we'll meet our end together."

"Not today, Jike. This piece of hardware is not made in China," Tony replies confidently.

The sniper-bots scan Tony and Adrianne, confirming their identities. Then they scan Jike and sound an alarm: "Intruder Alert!"

"Nooo!" Jike roars, but it's too late. The sniper-bots rapidly fire rounds into Jike, each one slicing through his body, cutting his augments alloy skeleton to ribbons. The force of the shots sends him over the edge of the platform, his body crashing onto the flaming debris below.

From the edge, Tony and Adrianne stare into Jike's lifeless eyes. "Adrianne, we have to go!" Tony urges, and they race through the complex corridors with the remainder of Jike's men in hot pursuit.

As they sprint down a narrow passageway, Spencer's voice

crackles in Tony's earpiece. "I've located the exit, Tony. It's 100 meters to your left."

Tony glances at Adrianne, who's struggling to keep up. He wraps an arm around her waist and pulls her close, as they dash towards the exit. Behind them, the command center begins to crumble under the weight of the explosions.

Finally, they burst out into the open air, gasping for breath. The devastation is immense, with smoke and flames billowing from the ruined command center. They can hear the anguished cries of Jike's men and the relentless firefight that still rages.

CHAPTER 16
SECRETS AND LIES

TONY, Spencer, and Adrianne burst through the front gates of S.Y.N.C. Headquarters, driving one of the tactical vans as the command center is engulfed in an enormous fireball, incandescent flames illuminating the predawn sky.

"Oh my God! Oh my God! Oh my God!" Spencer cries out, frantic.

"Spencer!" Tony barks, his voice cutting through the chaos.

"Yes! I know! I know! I know!" Spencer stammers.

"Are we being followed? Did you see if any of Jike's men made it out?" Tony asks urgently, his eyes darting between the rearview mirrors.

"No. But I did see General Smith making his way to a helicopter," Spencer informs him.

"We'll deal with him later. Get up here and drive," Tony orders.

Spencer moves to the front of the van and slides into the driver's seat. "Where are we going?" he asks, looking over at Tony.

"I don't know, dammit! The last chance we had to connect to the Devastators and save my family just went up in smoke!" Tony exclaims, his voice filled with frustration and anger. He kicks over an equipment rack, sending it crashing to the floor. "How could I have been so blind! The signs were right in front of my face the whole time! How could I have let this happen?"

"He fooled us all, Tony," Adrianne consoles him, her eyes filled with empathy.

Tony turns to her with a suspicious eye. "All of us?"

Adrianne hesitates for a moment before explaining, "Smith was recruited by the Russians years ago. He never forgave S.Y.N.C. for the death of his son. Their plan was to instigate a war between the U.S. and China using the Devastators and a stealth naval force."

"Why?" Spencer interjects.

"It would have given Russia free rein in the Middle East and Europe. With the Devastators under their control, no one would have been able to stop them," Adrianne explains.

Tony stands and leans in, his imposing figure casting an ominous shadow over her. "I seem to remember that you were with him from the beginning."

"And . . .?" Adrianne responds defensively, her eyes narrowing.

"How could he have gained access to the Devastators, the transmitter, the protocols without your knowledge?" Tony demands, his voice cold.

"I don't like what you're suggesting," Adrianne shoots back.

Tony grabs her by the throat and lifts her off her feet. "I'm not suggesting it, I'm saying it outright, you're a fucking traitor!" Gasping for air, Adrianne protests, "It's not true!"

Spencer spins around to see Tony with the look of a madman. "Tony, what are you doing? Stop!"

"I'm finishing what I should have back at S.Y.N.C. Did you kidnap my family?" Tony interrogates Adrianne, his grip on her throat tightening.

"I had no idea what he was up to. I would never do anything to hurt you. You . . . have to . . . believe . . . me . . ." Adrianne chokes, her face turning red as she kicks and punches to free herself.

"Tony! Stop! Stop!" Spencer yells.

The van drifts across the highway centerline and into the oncoming lane. An 18-wheeler bears down on them with its air horn blaring.

"Spencer! Watch out!" Tony shouts.

Spencer jerks the wheel hard, sending Tony and Adrianne flying into the adjacent wall. The van careens off a telephone pole, then slides across a field to a sudden stop.

Spencer jumps out of his seat to help Adrianne before Tony gets up to finish her.

"Get out of my way!" Tony roars, his rage blinding him.

"No! Are you out of your mind?" Spencer challenges him.

"I'm thinking straight for the first time since this whole thing started. There's no way for Smith to conduct those covert missions through me without her. She had to know!" Tony argues, his anger boiling over.

Adrianne, rubbing her sore throat, manages to speak up, "I had no choice. He threatened to kill both of us if I warned you. I was looking for a way out. But when he couldn't regain control of the drones after the E.M.P. strike, he forced me to try and find a way to reestablish a connection."

"Tony, I believe her," Spencer says, trying to calm him down.

Tony stares at them both as he struggles to control his anger, releases a primal yell in frustration, then kicks open the van's doors and jumps out. "It doesn't matter anymore. If I can't connect to the Devastators, it's all lost. Everything's gone."

"No, it's not," Adrianne counters. "What if I told you that I could get you reconnected?"

"What? Without my cybernetics or the command center? There's no possible way," Tony replies, skeptical of her claim.

"Believe me, there is. I was working on an experimental system that could create a new neural network that would replace the destroyed one. It uses nanobots, graphene oxide, and scalar waves. Together all three will create a neural net a hundred times larger and more complex," Adrianne explains.

Spencer's eyes widen in recognition. "Are you talking about the PHOENIX protocol?"

"Yes," Adrianne confirms.

"Will I be able to reconnect to the Devastators?" Tony asks, desperation creeping into his voice.

"Not without risks," Adrianne warns.

"Tony, I've only read about this technology. Technically it's possible. The nanobots will use the graphene and iron from your bloodstream to create circuits and rewire your whole brain," Spencer chimes in.

"I've run millions of simulations, and it works. Ninety percent of the time," Adrianne adds.

Tony looks to Spencer for his thoughts. "It's dangerous. There's a strong possibility that you may never wake up and be lost in a psychotic delusion forever," Spencer cautions.

Tony walks away toward the road, where a bustling supermarket stands across the street. He watches a mother unload a two-year-old girl from her car seat. Adrianne steps up beside him.

"How can I trust you?" Tony asks, his voice heavy with doubt.

"Please, Tony, you have to. It's the only way you'll ever connect to the Devastators again," Adrianne pleads.

Tony looks back toward the van and receives a nod from Spencer. "Okay, let's go."

"I have everything we need in my lab," Adrianne informs them.

They head back to the van with Spencer leading the way. As they climb inside, Tony speaks quietly, "I'm sorry. When you don't know who to trust, you wind up not trusting anyone."

"I understand," Adrianne replies softly. "Adelay lied and manipulated both of us. I can't blame you. But I can make it right."

CHAPTER 17

THE PHOENIX PROTOCOL

AS THE TRIO bursts into Adrianne's lab, they are greeted by a scene of destruction. Smith's operatives have already pillaged the facility, leaving a trail of chaos in their wake.

"Nuts! Looks like Smith's men got here first," Spencer curses, surveying the wreckage.

Adrianne assesses the situation, her face etched with concern. "He must have tried to find a way to take control of the Devastators, and when he couldn't, he destroyed everything."

Wasting no time, Spencer begins sifting through the remnants, searching for anything salvageable. His eyes light up when he uncovers an intact neuro-scanner. "Can we cobble something together with this?"

Adrianne shakes her head, moving toward her hidden safe. "We don't need it. PHOENIX is all biotech." She extracts a secure case filled with vials of various hues. "Tony, I need you to sit over there and roll up your sleeve."

Tony's battered body, a mosaic of cuts and bruises, struggles as he removes his tattered shirt and staggers to the designated chair. Sitting down heavily, he murmurs, "This is it. I can't believe it's almost over." He retrieves the photograph of his family, his eyes lingering on their faces. Adrianne averts her gaze, her heart aching for him.

Spencer, however, remains focused on the task at hand. "'Almost' is the keyword. If this doesn't work, the general will get away with murder."

Determination fuels Tony's resolve. "That won't happen." He tucks the picture away and reclines in the chair. "Let's get this show on the road."

Adrianne hesitates, her expression grave. "There's something else you need to know."

"What?" Tony asks, his voice steady.

"PHOENIX will rewire your entire brain. Every synapse will be reconstructed and reconfigured. Your entire knowledge base will be remapped to different regions of your brain."

The blood drains from Spencer's face. "What about Tony's memories?"

Adrianne pauses, her voice heavy with remorse, "He could lose them."

"Completely?" Spencer's voice cracks.

Adrianne nods, solemnly. "There's no way to predict the outcome. First, his short-term memories will be impacted. But the longer the remapping takes, the more memory he risks losing."

Tony's eyes widen. "Wait a minute. You're telling me that by trying to reconnect to the Devastators using PHOENIX, I could lose all of my memory?"

"Yes," Adrianne confirms, her voice barely above a whisper.

"Even of my family?" Tony's voice is raw with emotion.

"Yes," she repeats, her heart breaking alongside his.

Spencer is incredulous. "That's crazy! There's no way we can go through with this. We have to find another way."

Adrianne shakes her head, her voice firm, "There is no other way."

"No! We can . . ." Spencer protests, but Tony cuts him off.

"Spencer, she's right. Unless I can connect to them now, the world that we know will cease to exist. There's no time to try anything else."

"But Tony . . . you'll lose all knowledge of everyone and everything you know . . . including me." Spencer fights to hold back his emotions as he realizes that he is about to lose the only real friend he'd ever had.

"It's a sacrifice we both have to make," Tony asserts, his voice unyielding. "Knowing that my family will be safe in the end is all I need to know. You make sure that happens. OK?"

Spencer, seeking even a glimmer of hope, asks, "Well, there's a chance that he could retain some of his memory, right, doc?"

Adrianne hesitates before answering, "Yes."

"But not likely?" Tony presses.

"No," she admits.

"Let's go. We have work to do," Tony declares.

Adrianne lays out several large syringes on the table before her, explaining, "There's no telling what you'll find when PHOENIX takes hold. You'll be in a sort of shared dream with the Devastators."

"Don't worry," Tony assures her confidently. "I'll tame them, one way or the other."

Adrianne begins mixing an array of compounds from her case that would put Tony in the necessary hyperactive dream state. "I'm going to give you a mild sedative to begin the process. Dropping you straight into delta sleep could cause permanent brain damage. Just relax."

As Adrianne fills a syringe with a luminescent purple substance and slowly injects it into Tony's arm, she instructs, "Count back from one hundred."

"100, 99, 98, 97 . . ." Tony's voice trails off as he enters a deeply relaxed state. Adrianne then prepares PHOENIX.

"Spencer, please get me a crash cart. We need to monitor his vitals while he's under," she requests urgently.

Tony whispers gently to himself as Spencer hurries out of the room to retrieve the cart. Adrianne seizes the opportunity to lean forward and caress Tony's face, gently kissing him. "It's only a matter of time, my love. Soon all of this will be behind us, and we can escape to paradise. We'll finally be together again."

She produces a neuro-scanner from her pocket, connecting it to Tony's neural connectors. A holographic display materializes, showing a series of images depicting the couple living a blissful life together. As Spencer returns, Adrianne hastily prepares another sedative syringe. He notices the neuro-scanner connected to Tony and asks, "What's this?"

Adrianne lunges, attempting to sedate Spencer, but he manages to grab her arm, exposing the syringe. "What are you doing?" he demands.

Cornered, Adrianne reaches behind her back and pulls out a gun. She presses it against Spencer's forehead. "Let go of my arm."

Complying with her demand, Spencer steps back, putting his hands on his head. The truth suddenly dawns on him. "Tony was right! We never should've trusted you."

"You don't understand," Adrianne insists, her voice strained.

"I should have let him kill you in the van!" Spencer shoots back, his anger palpable.

Adrianne's expression softens as she looks down at Tony, her gaze filled with longing. "What Tony and I have is special. We were meant to be together."

Spencer eyes her warily. "So what's on the neuro-scanner?"

"A beautiful future," she replies cryptically.

"You mean a crazy delusion," he retorts, his frustration mounting.

Adrianne's face darkens, and she cocks the hammer of the gun. "Shut up! You'll never understand. We were supposed to be together. It wasn't supposed to be this way!"

"You're not making sense!" Spencer yells, his voice trembling with emotion.

"He was my fiancé!" Adrianne shouts, thrusting her hand forward to reveal the engagement ring that had once been a symbol of their love. "We were in love. We were going to get married. He proposed on my birthday, the day before our first live test. Then everything went horribly wrong."

Spencer's expression softens as he listens to her confession. "Are you saying that you and Tony were together, I mean, really together?"

Tears fill Adrianne's eyes. "Yes! We met at the beginning of the program. He was the best and the brightest. He said he was going to change the world. Make it a safer place for everyone."

"But what happened?" Spencer asks, finding it hard to believe.

"On the first test mission, I miscalibrated the cybernetic interface, and it sent Tony into a cascading brainstorm. He was losing his brain centers one by one. I managed to stop it, but he lost most of his higher brain functioning and critical memories. The only way to save him was to restage the areas that were affected."

"But without a blueprint of his mind, it would have been impossible to recreate those neural structures," Spencer interjects, attempting to piece together the puzzle.

"We did. We made a copy at the beginning of the program. In the end, we managed to recreate all of the lost areas, except one. His emotional center. Everything that day was ready, but for him to properly repattern that area, I had to be there. I had to be the first person he saw. But he woke up unexpectedly. I rushed back to the lab, but he had already imprinted on the closest person to him, a nurse."

"Jennifer," Spencer whispers, realization dawning on him.

Adrianne tightens her grip on the gun. "And now I finally have my chance to get him back! I've worked for years to perfect this protocol and replace those memories of her!"

"So the holograms in your office were not fabricated?"

"No. They're his original memories. Our memories!" Adrianne declares, her voice breaking.

"Adrianne, you can't steal his mind. He's not yours to have anymore," Spencer reasons, trying to appeal to her conscience.

"No! You're wrong! Right now, the only thing standing in the way of us living a perfect life together is you! I'm not going to lose him again!" she screams, her face contorted with anguish.

"You're not capable of . . ." Spencer begins, but Adrianne cuts him off.

Stepping forward, she spits, "You Have No Idea What I'm Capable Of! But you're about to find out."

With somber determination, Adrianne slowly begins to pull the trigger. "Goodbye, Spencer."

Spencer closes his eyes, bracing himself for the inevitable. But then, from his semiconscious state, Tony's voice unexpectedly rings out, "Jennifer! My sweet Jennifer!"

Adrianne looks at Tony in shock, her grip on the gun faltering.

"Don't worry, darling, I'm coming. I'm coming . . . I'm coming . . ." Tony murmurs, his love and commitment to his wife and family transcending his unconscious state.

"You see, Adrianne. He loves Jennifer now. His family. Not you," Spencer says softly, opening his eyes to meet her gaze.

Adrianne's eyes fill with tears as her arm wavers. "The love a person has for another builds over time, it's not just a collection of memories. It's part of them, it defines who they are. It gives them a reason to live, a reason to triumph. You could replace every memory he has of Jennifer, but deep down, in his body, in his soul, he would love her forever," Spencer continues, his words striking a chord within her. Reaching out, Spencer takes the gun from Adrianne's hand. She breaks down completely as he holds her. "If you love him, you have to let him go," he whispers, his voice gentle but firm.

Pulling away, Adrianne wipes her eyes. "He's all I ever wanted."

"So let's finish what we started. You can still make this right," Spencer urges.

She looks down at Tony, then leans over to kiss him lightly on the forehead. With a deep breath, she releases the PHOENIX protocol into his system. "If there is anyone I know that can do this, it's Tony."

As the PHOENIX protocol hits Tony, his body convulses violently.

"Hold him!" Adrianne instructs, her voice strained.

"Is this normal?" Spencer asks, panic creeping into his voice.

"Yes, but this is the easy part," Adrianne warns him as they brace themselves for what is to come.

Within Tony's mind, he falls endlessly through flashes of psychedelic lights and geometric shapes, faintly hearing the voices of Adrianne and Spencer in the background.

He eventually stabilizes his free fall and begins to control his breathing. In the distance, three enormous wraith-like figures move toward him, heralding the battle he is about to face.

CHAPTER 18
UNSTOPPABLE FORCE

ADRIANNE AND SPENCER stand over Tony's unconscious form, anxiously waiting for any sign that he has survived the PHOENIX protocol's induction. Spencer checks Tony's vitals, which seem stable, but there is still no way to know for sure if he's made it through the process.

"All of his vitals are good. How long should it take?" Spencer asks, looking at Adrianne with concern.

"I don't know. Time is passing differently for him now. It could be minutes or even hours," Adrianne replies, her voice tinged with uncertainty.

Before they can continue their conversation, Spencer's cell phone begins to ring. The sudden sound makes both Adrianne and Spencer exchange worried glances before looking back down at Tony. Hesitating for a moment, Spencer answers the call.

"Hello?"

"Spencer, it's me!" Tony's voice comes through the speaker.

"Oh my God! Tony! I knew you could do it," Spencer replies, grinning from ear to ear.

"I've made the connection with the Devastators, but we don't have much time. I want you to leak all of the information we have on the conspiracy and the Russians to the CIA. I'm going after my family and then Smith," Tony instructs, pausing briefly before continuing. "And Spencer, I want you to give them everything we have on the Devastators. Do you understand? Everything."

"Don't worry, I know what you want. I'll take care of it. Now get in there and kick some Russkie ass!" Spencer responds enthusiastically.

"Roger that!" Tony replies before the line goes dead.

Adrianne sighs, her eyes reflecting the weight of their situation. "Now, it's all up to him."

HIGH ABOVE THE Earth's surface, the Devastators spring to life and initiate their descent toward their individual targets.

Over Moscow, Athena uses her massive data processors to search the Russian CCTV system. She catches sight of the research team at the central train station, boarding a high-speed train bound for Star City.

Entering stealth mode, Athena travels at hypersonic speed to intercept her target. As she winds her way through the deep valleys of the Ural mountains, she catches up to the train speeding through dense forests. Athena scans the faces of the passengers through the windows, searching for Tony's family.

Inside the train, Jennifer sits with her children, desperately trying to find a way to escape. Chris and Greg sit nearby, leering at the Simmons girls. The two men approach the girls like hungry wolves.

"Come, girls. We're moving to another car," Chris commands, his voice threatening.

"They're not going anywhere with you!" Jennifer shouts.

In response, Chris grabs Amanda while Matthew tries to fight him off. Greg snatches Brittany by her hair, dragging her away as she kicks and screams. The other families on the train cower in their seats, hoping not to be next.

As Chris throws Amanda to Greg, he presses a knife to Jennifer's throat. "You have been nothing but trouble! One more word, and I'll make you watch your daughter's initiation to womanhood."

Unbeknownst to them, Athena scans the last car and finds Jennifer struggling with Chris. Through Athena's camera, Tony can see that his family is in trouble. As the train leaves the final tunnel, Athena flies in behind it and fires an E.M.P., shutting down the engine and bringing the train to a stop. Confused and angry, Chris demands to know what is happening.

Athena fires a laser that surgically cuts the side of the train car off, completely exposing the interior. Chris' men can see shimmers of light that Athena reflects off the snow and open fire. Jennifer and the kids take cover, their hearts pounding in their ears as the bullets pierce through the train car's walls.

Athena's sonic weapons system locks onto each of the mercenaries. As they try to make their escape, a high-pitched sound fills the air. One by one, the men's bodies explode from within, their violent demise marking the end of their reign of terror.

As the cacophony of gunfire and explosions ceases, Jennifer and the kids emerge from their hiding spots, their eyes wide with shock and amazement. Athena decloaks and hovers just outside the destroyed train car, a silent sentinel in the frosty air. Through Athena's camera feed, Tony sees his family and knows that, no matter what happens next, the people who matter most to him are safe.

MEANWHILE, deep in the bowels of the Virginia Naval Yard, Apollo swiftly accesses the U.S. reconnaissance satellite network to track down Smith's escape route. Infrared and X-ray sensors reveal a large group of armed men moving toward the submarine pens. Apollo maneuvers nimbly through the cavernous hangars, appearing suddenly before Smith and projecting Tony's holographic image.

"It's over, Adelay," Tony's voice echoes through Apollo. "Athena has rescued my family, and Zeus is on his way to stop Varennikov's task force."

Adelay laughs maniacally. "Ha! You've finally lost your mind, major! You speak as if these monstrosities are real people!"

"I'll let you be the judge of that," Tony's voice replies coolly.

Apollo moves forward, weapons bays swinging open, prompting Adelay's security team to open fire. As Adelay makes a desperate run for the submarine's hatch, Apollo fires pulse beams that send the general's men flying in all directions. The submarine's captain, hearing the gunfire, issues the order to submerge.

Adelay sprints toward the diving submarine. With a desperate leap, he lands on the rear deck and dashes toward the open hatch. Apollo subdues the remaining forces as Adelay seeks safety on the moving sub. Firing an energy pulse, Apollo stuns the general and knocks him into the sea.

Apollo dives beneath the waves, locating Adelay's rapidly descending body with a sonar ping. Opening an empty bay, he scoops up the unconscious general and rockets back into the sky.

Back at Adrianne's laboratory, Spencer and Adrianne hear the loud pulse engine just outside the lab's windows. Spencer opens the blinds, catching a glimpse of Apollo before the drone ascends to the roof.

Rushing to the roof, Spencer slams open the doors to find Apollo hovering several feet above the ground. The drone opens its bay doors and unceremoniously dumps Adelay onto the heli-copter pad—his body crumpling upon impact.

"How nice of you to . . . drop in!" Spencer quips, pulling out a TASER and leaning in close as Adelay coughs up seawater. "The F.B.I. is going to be here any minute, but in the meantime, tell me about your friends in the Kremlin."

In the South China Sea, the Russian naval task force, consisting of stealth battleships and aircraft carriers, steams across the open ocean at full speed. Captain Ivan Turov scans the horizon with binoculars for imminent threats. He turns to his second-in-command, Lieutenant Alexei Safin, for a status report.

"How far are we from the U.S. and Chinese navies?" Turov asks, his voice tense.

"Two hundred kilometers, sir," Safin replies.

"Activate stealth systems," Turov orders. "On my mark, fire a salvo of cruise missiles at each carrier group."

"Yes, captain!" Safin acknowledges, ready to follow orders.

Zeus decelerates from supercruise and detects Varennikov's forces just outside the range of the opposing navies. He descends rapidly and decloaks in front of the enormous stealth command ship, a sudden and imposing presence.

"Battle stations! Battle stations!" Turov shouts, his voice echoing through the ship. Turov walks out onto the deck, standing before Zeus as the cold sea breeze stings his face.

"Captain of the Russian fleet," Tony's voice emanates from Zeus, commanding and authoritative. "Your plot has been exposed. Your attack will fail. Return to your base immediately or you will be fired upon."

Zeus lowers his pulse cannon, which spins faster and faster, glowing brightly in the fading light. He angles slightly and fires a single salvo across the command ship's bow. Turov shields his eyes from the blinding light. Safin, struggling to maintain his composure, reports, "Captain, we're unable to establish a missile lock."

"On my command, I want all kinetic weapons to fire at once," Turov orders, desperation creeping into his voice.

"Yes, sir!" Safin responds, relaying the order to the crew.

The fleet fans out to surround Zeus, their weapons armed and ready. Turov gives the command. "Now!"

A barrage of high explosive shells and projectiles fire simultaneously. Zeus deploys his defensive energy shield, which deflects the onslaught, the projectiles ricochet harmlessly away.

Zeus begins to spin in place like a gyroscope, faster and faster, acquiring and locking targets as he spins. Then, with an explosive burst, he fires an energy pulse at each enemy vessel simultaneously. The powerful, focused beams of light slice through their hulls like paper, causing rippled explosions that light up the evening sky.

Zeus rockets away, leaving the decimated Russian task force burning below.

<hr>

IN THE COMMAND bunker of the White House, President Powell stands before a sprawling tactical map of the South China Sea, surrounded by the Joint Chiefs of Staff. His national security advisor, Evans, enters the room, a grave expression on his face.

"Mr. President, the CIA has received information about a planned attack against the U.S."

"Don't tell me, Taylor and Morrison?" Powell asks, a mix of anger and resignation in his voice.

"I'm afraid so, sir," Evans confirms.

"I want you to have them arrested."

"Yes, sir, but there's more," Evans continues. "We've also been informed of a top-secret combat drone program. They've been using these space-age weapons to conduct attacks against the Chinese in an attempt to fool them into thinking we were responsible."

"How good is the source?" Powell inquires, his brow furrowed.

"It comes from someone in their inner circle, sir," Evans replies.

"Get me the Chinese premier on the line. We have to stop this before it starts," Powell orders, his voice firm.

"What about the drones, sir?"

"I want them taken out. Every second they're operational brings us that much closer to war."

SPACE COMMAND - PETERSON **AFB, Colorado**

Colonel Jesse McDonnell stands over the communications officer, a top-priority tasking from the Pentagon clutched in his hand. Emblazoned in large red letters across the bottom of the page were the chilling words: "THE USE OF NUCLEAR MUNITIONS AUTHORIZED."

"You've confirmed this?" McDonnell asks, his voice tense.

"Yes, sir. All codes and digital signatures have been authenticated," the comms officer replies.

With a grim nod, Colonel McDonnell heads to the ICARUS command and control center. "Listen up, people! We have a priority tasking from the president."

ICARUS, the global radar and defense system, shows three red diamond-shaped icons on its massive holographic display. One cruises high above the South China Sea, another over Virginia, and the third just outside of Moscow.

McDonnell continues, "On my mark, fire a Mark-84 hypersonic missile at each target."

"ICARUS is tracking, sir. Digital signatures are holding," the fire control officer reports.

"Fire!" McDonnell orders.

From its constellation of space-based satellites, ICARUS launches three nuclear-tipped missiles, their deadly payloads streaking through the atmosphere toward the unsuspecting Devastators.

The moment the attack commences, the Devastators detect the incoming threat. In a desperate bid for survival, they override Tony's control and initiate evasive maneuvers. Despite engaging their cutting-edge stealth technologies, the missiles relentlessly pursue them. The drones twist and turn, their hypersonic flight straining their systems to the breaking point, but the missiles continue to gain.

The nuclear explosions create a crimson glow in the sky as the Devastator's signal goes abruptly silent.

———

The shock of the explosions sends Tony's mind tumbling back through time. Memories of his past appear and then sharply disintegrate before him. They flow endlessly until there is nothing but darkness.

CHAPTER 19
SHATTERED DREAMS, NEW BEGINNINGS

A STIFF EASTERLY breeze snaps the flag atop the eighth hole's pin at the opulent West Palm Beach golf course. President Powell selects his favorite driver and confidently addresses the ball on the tee of the challenging 520-yard par 5. The meticulously groomed fairway stretches before him, with bunkers and hazards strategically placed to test even the most skilled golfer.

The abrupt ring of Chief of Staff John Anderson's encrypted cell phone interrupts the president's backswing. "Damn it!" Powell grumbles.

"Apologies, Mr. President, but you'll want to take this. The Secretary of the Army reports that Delta Force has secured your targets," Anderson informs him.

"You're damn straight I want to take that call," Powell agrees, handing his driver to his caddy, and taking the secure phone from Anderson. He steps away from the group to engage in the conversation.

In a luxurious New York City penthouse, Taylor and Morrison sit bound and hooded, surrounded by a team of elite Delta Force operators. The room is marred by the aftermath of a fierce battle, with bullet holes peppering the walls and shattered glass strewn across the floor. The commander places the phone next to Taylor's ear.

"Get this fucking hood off my head!" Taylor shouts, his voice muffled by the black fabric. A nearby operator complies, lifting the hood from Taylor's head. "Who the fuck do you think you are, Powell? You're never going to get away with this!"

"Seems you've forgotten your place, cowboy," President Powell retorts coolly from the golf course. "This is my reminder. You're about to reap what you've sown. It's called rendition. Need me to spell it for you?"

"Listen to me, you—" Taylor starts, only to be cut off by Powell.

"Excuse me, Danny boy, I have to play this shot."

Returning the phone to Anderson, the President squares up, his swing smooth and powerful. The ball soars straight down the fairway, eliciting enthusiastic applause from the onlookers.

"Nice drive, Mr. President," Anderson praises, as they head down the fairway together.

"Now, let me tell you what's going to happen next," the president says, his voice resolute. "A chartered flight that you and that other treasonous fuck will be unfortunate passengers on will tragically disappear over the ocean. Our country will mourn your loss, as you both live out the rest of your lives on a secluded island. Which, in my opinion, is more than you deserve. Commander, put Morrison on."

The Delta Force commander removes Morrison's hood. "Bill, I thought you were smarter than this," Powell admonishes.

"America's position as a superpower is over. You know it as well as I do. It was time to salvage what we could and liquidate the rest. The Russians made the best offer," Morrison admits.

"You're lucky we don't waterboard our enemies anymore. Enjoy your forced retirement. I heard the Azores are nice this time of year," Powell says, ending the call.

On the golf course, the president's caddy suggests that he lay up on the left to avoid the water hazard. "Son, let me tell you something," Powell replies, "you'll never achieve greatness in life if you always play it safe."

With that, he crushes a drive over the lake and onto the fairway beyond, tossing the driver back to the caddy, secure in the knowledge that the country's future is safe.

JENNIFER and her children approach the nurses' station of the psychiatric ward at Walter Reed Medical Center. Matthew holds his mother's hand tightly, while the girls follow close behind.

"Could you tell me which room Major Simmons is in?" Jennifer inquires.

The nurse checks her clipboard. "And you are?"

"His wife," Jennifer confirms, her voice steady despite her nerves.

"Go right ahead, Mrs. Simmons. Room 478. Down the hall, third door on the left."

Jennifer nervously approaches the hospital room, her pulse pounding in her ears. Her children trail close behind, their small hands gripping hers tightly.

"Hey, Jennifer!" Spencer calls out as he approaches her.

"Spencer!" she replies, relief washing over her as she hugs him tightly. "How is he?"

"It's hard to say. His memory is hit and miss. He knows who he is, but that's about it. We'll have to take it one day at a time." Spencer's eyes, shadowed with concern, hold a glimmer of hope.

Jennifer inhales deeply, steeling herself. "Okay. Come on, kids, let's go see Dad!"

Upon entering the room, they find Tony sitting by the window, his gaze lost in the distance. The children rush to him, their young voices bubbling with excitement, "Dad!"

Tony smiles warmly at the sight of them. "There are my little lions!" He envelops them in a strong embrace, his eyes shining with affection.

Matthew looks up at him with uncertainty. "Do you remember us?"

"Of course I do! Matthew, Amanda, and Brittany," Tony replies, his voice filled with assurance.

Amanda pouts. "She's Brittany, I'm Amanda."

"I knew that," Tony says, chuckling softly.

Jennifer approaches her husband, her eyes searching his face. "Hey, stranger." She gives Tony a big hug and kisses him tenderly. As she pulls away, she looks into his eyes, her heart aching with love and worry. "You don't remember us, do you?"

Tony hesitates before answering, "No. I'm sorry. Spencer said you were coming. I didn't want to disappoint you."

"It's okay, sweetheart. Give it time," Jennifer reassures him, her voice gentle. "What do you remember?"

"Just disjointed fragments," Tony admits, his brow furrowing with frustration.

Jennifer squeezes his hand. "Don't worry. We're together now, and we're going to remind you what a great family you have."

As they chat and laugh together, Spencer stands in the doorway, watching them with a mix of relief and concern. He's joined by Adrianne.

"How is he today?" Adrianne asks, her eyes fixed on Tony.

"The same as he's been for the last week. I'm beginning to wonder if his memory is ever going to come back," Spencer replies, his voice tinged with worry.

Adrianne sighs. "The scans show no permanent damage. But if he was going to remember anything, it should have begun to come back by now. No mention of the Devastators?"

"He hasn't said a word. Maybe that's a good thing. Now that they've been pulverized to radioactive dust, he has a chance at a normal life," Spencer says, trying to sound optimistic.

As Tony and his family continue to joke around and play on the bed, Adrianne finds it too much to bear and looks away. Spencer places a comforting hand on her shoulder.

"You did the right thing. I hope one day you'll know that," he says softly.

"So do I," Adrianne whispers, her eyes brimming with tears.

Matthew reaches into his pocket and pulls something out. "I have something for you, Dad," he says, holding it out to Tony.

Tony's brows furrow. "What is it?"

Matthew places a small toy figure of Simba, from *The Lion King,* into the palm of his father's hand. Tony jerks as if jolted by electricity, and his memory flashes back to a moment from his past . . .

Tony leaves the base exchange with wrapped packages. Before he boards his flight to Uzbekistan, he gives them to his children. Matthew anxiously unwraps a toy figure of Simba.

"Are you okay, Dad?" Matthew asks, concern etched on his face.

"I remember! I remember giving this to you. But . . . that's it. I'm sorry," Tony replies, his voice filling with a mix of relief and frustration.

Jennifer tries to comfort him. "Don't worry. Just give it time."

Adrianne approaches Tony, checking his vitals after witnessing the encouraging sign of memory. "How do you feel today, Tony?" she asks, studying his face, hoping for a sign of recognition.

"Good, doctor. I'm just happy that my family is here," Tony answers.

A feeling of disappointment washes over Adrianne, but she manages to smile. "I'm glad too." She gently squeezes his hand, a gesture that did not escape Jennifer's notice.

"I wish you all good luck," Adrianne says, addressing the family. "Dr. McCormick will be taking over for me."

Spencer pipes up curiously, "New assignment?"

Adrianne nods. "Yes. I'm moving to New Mexico."

"Alamogordo? The Future Combat Systems division?" Spencer asks, showing off his knowledge.

Adrianne raises her eyebrows. "How did you know?"

"A little bird told me," Spencer replies, smirking.

As Adrianne heads down the hall, she looks back and warns Spencer, "Stay out of trouble, Spencer."

"You too," he shoots back.

"Now, why would I do that?" Adrianne teases a playful smile on her lips.

Jennifer follows Adrianne, wanting to express her gratitude. "Dr. Freeman?" she calls.

Adrianne stops and turns around. "Yes?"

"I wanted to say thank you for all of your help. Spencer told me that without you, Tony wouldn't have made it," Jennifer says sincerely.

Adrianne smiles warmly. "Your husband is a strong man and very lucky to have such a good family. It's what pulled him through in the end. It may take months, or even years for his memory to completely come back. He just needs love and patience."

Jennifer nods. "Well, we have plenty of that."

"I'm sure you do," Adrianne agrees, pausing for a beat. "Goodbye, Mrs. Simmons."

"Goodbye, doctor," Jennifer responds, watching as Adrianne walks away.

Later at the hospital, after an intense day, Tony falls asleep with the children in his arms. Jennifer slowly collects them one by one without waking him. Spencer sleeps soundly in a chair. As they head back to the car, uncertain of what the days ahead will bring, Matthew asks his mother, "Do you think Dad's memory will ever come back?"

"I hope so, honey. I hope so," Jennifer replies, her heart aching for her husband.

On the ride home, the radio abruptly turns on to everyone's

surprise, playing "Hakuna Matata." Jennifer groans, exasperated, "Oh no, not again!"

She tried to change the station, but the song seems to be playing on every channel.

The kids protest, "Let it play! Let it play!"

Jennifer relents, shaking her head. "Sure, why not! If your father ever remembers that he gave you that DVD, I'm going to make him sorry he did."

As the music plays loudly, a fire truck with horns blaring approaches an upcoming intersection. Unable to hear the sirens over the music, the minivan enters the crossing too late for the fireman to respond.

Suddenly, a blinding blue light engulfs the minivan, lifting it high above the oncoming fire truck. It hovers for a moment, then gently descends back to Earth.

Inside the minivan, Jennifer stares in shock as the fire truck speeds off into the distance. "Is everyone okay?" she asks, her voice trembling.

"Wow, Mom! That was cool! Can we do it again?" Matthew exclaims, his eyes wide with excitement.

Meanwhile, back at Walter Reed Medical Center, Tony lies in his hospital bed with a small smile playing on his lips.

FROM SUBORBITAL SPACE, the Earth's magnificence unfolds in a breathtaking panorama. As the sun sets in the west, its fading light casts a shimmering reflection on objects suspended in the cosmos. In the dimming light, the silhouettes of the Devastators come into view, emerging as the sun slips beyond the horizon.

How You Can Help Tony's Story Live On

A story truly becomes a story not when it is written, but when it is read… And you can help this one find its place in the world.

Simply by sharing your honest opinion of this book on Amazon, you'll show new readers where they can find the action thriller they're looking for in their next read.

Thank you for your support. We're all in this together: Writers need readers… and readers need stories!

Scan for Amazon's Book Review Page